"Quit playing ring-around-a-rosy," Sergeant Holcomb said. "This is murder. Who is your client?"

Perry Mason shook his head. "That information is confidential."

"You'll become an accessory if you try to protect a murderer."

"I know. But my client will have to speak for himself. I'll have him at the district attorney's office at nine o'clock in the morning."

Holcomb regarded Mason with smoldering hostility. "All right," he said, "have it your own way. But remember this. Your client won't be entitled to one damned bit of consideration."

"We're not asking for consideration," Mason told him. "We're asking for our rights. And I think I know what they are."

Mason turned and walked out with Paul Drake, who wished he were as confident as Mason that they would be able to prove their client innocent of murder in **The Case of the Daring Decoy**, a particularly ingenious puzzler originally published by William Morrow and Company, Inc., at $2.95.

THE CASE OF THE
Daring Decoy
ERLE STANLEY GARDNER

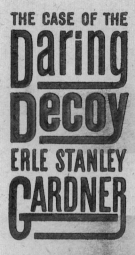

POCKET BOOKS, INC.
NEW YORK

THE CASE OF THE DARING DECOY

William Morrow edition published October, 1957

POCKET BOOK edition published April, 1960
1st printing .... February, 1960

L

POCKET BOOK editions are distributed in the U.S. by Affil-
iated Publishers, Inc., 630 Fifth Avenue, New York 20, N.Y.

FOREWORD

For the most part I have dedicated my Perry Mason books to outstanding figures in the field of legal medicine. But this book is dedicated to a doctor of medicine; one of the kindest, most considerate men I have ever met. He reached the top of the ladder in his chosen profession, and then, in place of taking up golf or yachting, turned his razor-keen mind to a "spare time" study of the problems of evidence, of law enforcement and the part the citizen could and should play in co-operating with the various law-enforcement agencies.

Merton M. Minter, M.D., is a Diplomate of the American Board of Internal Medicine, a member of the Board of Regents of the University of Texas, and, in fact, holds so many offices in the field of education, banking and medicine that there isn't room to list them here.

I am writing this because I wish more of the influential members of the medical profession would follow in Doctor Minter's steps. We need their sharp minds, their diagnostic skills, their seasoned judgment in the field of better law enforcement and the better administration of justice.

And so I dedicate this book to one of the most sympathetic, courteous, and thoughtful doctors in the world, a man who is rounding out his career doing good for his fellow man in the fields of medicine, education, law enforcement and justice, my friend,

MERTON MELROSE MINTER, M.D.

—Erle Stanley Gardner

CAST OF CHARACTERS

THE CASE OF THE
Daring Decoy

CHAPTER ONE

JERRY CONWAY opened the paper to page six.

There it was, just as it had been every day for the last week.

It was a half-page ad signed: PROXY HOLDERS BOARD OF SALVAGE, cleverly written, starting off with a statement that was manifestly true on the face of it:

You stockholders of the California & Texas Global Development & Exploration Company invested your money because you wanted to make money. You wanted money for yourselves, your children, and your heirs.

What are you getting?

Aside from a stroke of pure luck, what has Jerry Conway done for you? He says he is "pyramiding." He says he is "building." He says he is laying a "firm foundation."

That isn't the way the most expert operators in the business look at it.

These people say Jerry Conway is laying an egg.

You're entitled to a run for your money. You're entitled to action. You want to make a profit now, next year, and the year after, not ten years or twenty years from now.

Mail your proxy to Gifford Farrell, care Proxy Holders Board of Salvage, and then, with Giff Farrell in the saddle, watch things begin to hum.

Farrell believes in results, not promises. Farrell believes in action, not idle planning; in decisions, not daydreaming; in performing, not hoping.

Conway closed the paper. It was, he admitted to himself, an ad that would get proxies. The ad also hurt.

According to the Proxy Holders Board of Salvage, it was simply a stroke of luck that the C. & T. Global Development & Exploration Company had been right in the middle of the Turkey Ridge pool.

After that pool came in, Jerry Conway could have declared big dividends, pushed up the value of the stock. Instead he had chosen to put the money into other holdings potentially as big as the Turkey Ridge pool.

Gifford Farrell had been a disruptive influence from the start. Finally there had been a showdown before the board of directors, and Farrell had been thrown out. Now he had started a fight for proxies. He was trying to wrest control of the company away from Conway.

Who was back of Farrell? What money was paying for the ads in the papers? Conway wished he knew. He wished he knew how to strike back.

Conway's over-all, master plan had to be carried out quietly. The minute he tried to blueprint his plans, he defeated his own purpose. Prices of properties he hoped to acquire would go up beyond all reason.

Conway couldn't explain publicly. He intended to address the stockholders' meeting. He was hoping that the stockholders who were there, and most of the big ones would be, would stand by him. But what about the smaller stockholders? The ones who had put in a few dollars here, a few dollars there? Stockholders who concededly wanted profits and action?

Would these people stay in line, or would they send their proxies to Farrell?

An analysis of the books showed that there were enough

small stockholders to take over control, if they acted as a unit. If Farrell could get their proxies, they'd act as a unit. If, however, Giff Farrell's clever ads didn't get more than 60 per cent of these smaller stockholders, and if Conway's personality could hold the larger investors in line at the stockholders' meeting, everything would be all right.

Those, however, were two great big ifs. And at the moment Jerry Conway didn't have the answer.

Jerry Conway folded the newspaper, switched out lights in the office, and was heading for the door, when the phone rang.

Jerry answered it. He was answering all phone calls now. He dared take no chance of offending some of the small stockholders who would want explanations, and, heaven knows, there had been enough of them who had called up! So far, these people had listened to his explanation that a company in the process of acquiring valuable oil properties couldn't blueprint its plans in the public press. Stock that the investors had bought a year ago had more than doubled in value. Giff Farrell said that was due purely to a "stroke of luck" with which Conway had nothing to do. Conway would always laugh when he quoted that. Stay with him and there might be more strokes of luck, he promised. Tie up with Giff Farrell's crowd, and the company would be looted for the benefit of insiders.

So Jerry Conway picked up the telephone.

"Jerry Conway speaking," he said.

The woman's voice was intriguing, and yet there was something about it that carried its own warning. It was too syrupy-smooth, and Conway felt he had heard it before.

"Mr. Conway," she said, "I must see you. I have some secret information which will be of the greatest value to you."

"I'll be in my office at nine o'clock tomorrow morning, and—"

"No, no. I can't come to your office."

"Why not?"

"People are watching me."

"What do *you* suggest?"

"I want to meet you privately, alone, somewhere where no one will know, somewhere where we won't be disturbed."

"You have some idea?" Jerry asked.

"Yes, if you'll go to the Apex Motel out on Sunset tonight, register under your own name as a single, turn your lights out, leave your door unlocked, and wait until after midnight, I'll—"

"I'm sorry," Jerry interrupted. "That's out of the question."

"Why is it out of the question?"

"Well," Jerry equivocated, "I have other plans for this evening."

"How about tomorrow night?"

"No, I'm afraid I can't do it tomorrow night, either."

"Is it because you're afraid of me?"

"I'm living in a glass house at the present time," Conway said drily.

"Look," she said, "I can't talk with you any longer. My name is— Well, let's say it's Rosalind. Just call me Rosalind. I want to see you. I have information you should have, information that you *must* have in order to protect the stockholders, protect yourself, and save the company. Giff has a lot more proxies than you think he has. He's a very dangerous antagonist. You're going to have to start a counter campaign."

"I'm sorry," Conway said. "There are certain matters I can't discuss over the telephone, and certain matters I can't discuss in the press. After all, the stockholders must have some faith in someone. Otherwise, they'll wind up in the financial gutter. Their holdings have doubled in value during the past year under my management. I have every reason to believe they'll continue to climb, and—"

"Good heavens!" the voice exclaimed. "Don't try to sell *me*. I *know*. Giff Farrell is a crook. He's trying to get control of the company so he and his friends can make a cleanup by manipulating company assets. I wouldn't trust him two feet away for two seconds. I want you to have the information that I have."

"Can you put in a letter?" Conway asked, curious.

"No, I can't put it in a letter," she said impatiently, "and if you knew as much as I know, you'd realize that I'm in danger just talking to you."

"What danger?" he asked.

"In danger of getting killed," she said angrily, and slammed up the telephone.

Jerry Conway sat at his desk for some minutes after he had dropped the receiver into its cradle on the telephone. There had been something about the voice that had carried conviction.

However, Jerry knew the necessity for caution. Half a dozen attempts had been made to frame him during the last two weeks. If he should go to a motel, leave the door open, have some young woman join him in the dark, and then perhaps a few minutes later there should be the sound of police whistles and— No, it was a chance Jerry simply couldn't take. Even a little unpleasant newspaper notoriety coming at this time could well turn the tide in the proxy battle.

Jerry Conway waited for fifteen minutes, then again switched out the lights, saw that the night latch was on the door, and went down in the elevator.

Rosalind telephoned the next day at a little after eleven.

Jerry Conway's secretary said, "There's a woman on the line who gives the name of Rosalind and no other name.

She says you know her, that she has to talk with you, that it's important."

"I'll talk with her," Jerry said. He picked up the telephone, said, "Hello," and again heard the smooth tones of Rosalind's voice, a voice that he felt he should recognize but couldn't.

"Good morning, Mr. Conway."

"Good morning, Rosalind."

"Did you know you're being followed?"

Jerry hesitated. "I have wondered if perhaps certain people weren't taking an undue interest in my comings and goings."

"You're being tailed by a high-class detective agency," she said, "and that agency is being supplemented by a couple of thugs. Be very, very careful what you do."

"Thank you for the warning," Jerry said.

"But," she went on, "you *must* see me. I've tried to think of some way of getting in touch with you. One of the men who's shadowing you at the present time is a private detective. He's not dangerous. He's just doing a routine job of shadowing. However, there's another individual named Baker, whom they call Gashouse Baker. He's a one-man goon squad. Watch out for him! Are you armed?"

"Lord, no!" Conway said.

"Then get a permit to carry a gun," she said. "You shouldn't have too much trouble spotting the detective. Baker will be more difficult. At the moment, he's driving a beat-up, black car with a corner bent on the license plate. Don't take any chances with that man!

"These people are playing for keeps and they don't intend to play fair. You're looking for a straightforward battle for proxies and you're planning everything along those lines. These people don't play that way.

"And don't ever mention to anyone that you have been in communication with me. I shouldn't have given you the name of Rosalind, but I wanted to put the cards on the table."

Jerry Conway frowned thoughtfully. "I wish you could tell me something of the nature of the information you have, something—"

"Look," she said, "I can tell you the number of proxies they hold, and if I have your assurance that you can protect me, I can give you the names of the people who have sent in proxies. However, if any of this information should get out, they'd know where it came from and I'd be in danger."

"How much danger?" Jerry Conway asked. "If it's economic security that you—"

"Don't be silly!" she interrupted sarcastically. "I've seen one woman after Gashouse Baker worked her over. I—Oh-oh!"

The phone abruptly clicked and the connection went dead.

Jerry Conway gave the matter a great deal of thought. That noon he drove around in a somewhat aimless pattern, carefully watching cars in his rearview mirror. He couldn't be certain anyone was following him, but he became very uneasy. He felt he was in danger.

Conway knew that he was going to have to take a chance on Rosalind. If she had the information she said she had, it would be of inestimable value. If he knew the names of the persons who had sent in proxies, there would still be time to concentrate a campaign on those people.

Rosalind called shortly after two-thirty. This time there was a note of pleading and desperation in her voice.

"I *have* to get this information to you so you can act on it. Otherwise the company will be ruined."

"Exactly what is it that you want?"

"I want to give you information. I want primarily to keep Giff Farrell and his crowd of goons from wrecking

7

the company. I want to protect the honest investors, and I . . . I want to get even."

"With whom?"

"Use your imagination," she said.

"Now, look here," Conway said, "I can have a representative meet you. I can send someone in—"

She interrupted with a hollow laugh. "The business that I have with you is with you personally, with the number-one man in the company. I'm not taking any assurances from anyone else. If you're too cautious to meet me face to face to get this information, then I guess the things Giff Farrell is saying about you *are* true!"

Conway reached a sudden decision. "Call me back in fifteen minutes," he said. "I'm not free to make arrangements at the present time. Can you call in fifteen minutes? Will you talk with me then?"

"I'll call," she promised.

Conway summoned his secretary. "Miss Kane, the young woman who has just called me is going to call again in fifteen minutes. She's going to make arrangements with me for a meeting, a meeting which has to be held in the greatest secrecy.

"I want you to listen in on the conversation. I want you to make shorthand notes of exactly what is said so that if the necessity should arise, you can repeat that conversation verbatim."

Eva Kane never appeared surprised. She took things in her stride, with a calm, professional competence.

"Do you want shorthand notes of what *she* says, or shorthand notes of the entire conversation?"

"Notes of the entire conversation. Transcribe them as soon as you've taken them, and be in a position to swear to them if necessary."

"Very well, Mr. Conway," Eva Kane said, and left the office.

When the phone failed to ring at the end of the fifteen-minute period, Conway began restlessly pacing the floor.

Abruptly the telephone rang. Conway made a dive for the desk, picked up the receiver, said, "Yes?"

Eva Kane's calmly professional voice said, "A young woman on the line who says you are expecting the call. A Miss Rosalind."

"You ready, Miss Kane?" Conway asked.

"Yes, Mr. Conway."

"Put her on."

Rosalind's voice came over the line. "Hello, Mr. Conway?"

"Rosalind?"

"Yes. What's your answer?"

"Look here," Conway said, "I want to talk with you, but I'll have to take adequate precautions."

"Precautions against what?"

"Against some sort of a trap."

Her laugh was bitter. "You're childless, unmarried, thirty-six. You aren't responsible to anyone for your actions. Yet you worry about traps!

"Tonight at exactly five-thirty the private detective who is shadowing you goes off duty. Another one takes over for the night shift. They don't make contact. Sometimes the night man is late. Perhaps it can be arranged for him to be late tonight. At precisely one minute past five-thirty leave your office, get in your car. Start driving west on Sunset Boulevard. Turn at Vine. Turn left on Hollywood Boulevard. Go to Ivar. Turn right, and then start running signals. Go through signals just as the lights are changing. Keep an eye on your rearview mirror. Cut corners. Make certain you're not being followed. I think you can shake off your tail."

"And after that?" Conway asked.

"Now, listen carefully," she said. "After that, after you

are absolutely certain that you're not being followed, go to the Empire Drugstore on Sunset and LaBrea. There are three phone booths in that store. Go to the one farthest from the door, enter the booth and at precisely six-fifteen that phone will ring. Answer it.

"If you have been successful in ditching your shadows, you will be directed where to go. If you haven't ditched your shadows, the phone won't ring."

"You're making all this seem terribly cloak-and-dagger," Conway protested somewhat irritably. "After all, if you have any information that—"

"It *is* terribly cloak-and-dagger," she interrupted. "Do you want a list of the stockholders who already have sent in proxies?"

"Very much," he said.

"Then come and get it," she told him, and hung up.

A few minutes later, Eva Kane entered the office with impersonal, secretarial efficiency, and handed Conway type-written sheets.

"A transcript of the conversation," she said.

"Thank you," Jerry told her.

She turned, started for the door, paused, then suddenly whirled and came toward him. "You mustn't do it, Mr. Conway!"

He looked at her with some surprise.

"Oh, I know," she said, the words pouring out in rapid succession as though she were afraid he might be going to stop her. "You've never encouraged any personalities in the office. I'm only a piece of office machinery as far as you're concerned. But I'm human. I know what you're going through, and I want you to win out in this fight, and . . . and I know something about women's voices, and—" She hesitated over a word or two, then trailed off into silence as though her vocal mechanism had been a motor running out of fuel.

10

"I didn't know I was so unapproachable," Conway protested.

"You're not! You're not! Don't misunderstand me. It's only that you've always been impersonal. . . . I mean, you've kept things on a business basis. I know I'm speaking out of turn, but please, please don't do anything as ridiculous as this woman suggests."

"Why?" he asked.

"Because it's a trap."

"How do you know it's a trap?"

"It stands to reason if she had any information she wanted to give you, she could simply put it in an envelope, write your name on the envelope, put a stamp on the envelope, and drop it in the nearest mailbox."

Conway thought that over.

"All of this mystery, all of this cloak-and-dagger stuff, it's simply a trap."

Conway said gravely, "I can't take any chances on passing up this information."

"You mean you're going?"

"I'm going," he said doggedly. "You said something about her voice?"

She nodded.

"What about it?"

"I've trained my ears to listen to voices over the telephone. I was a phone operator for two years. There's something about her voice . . . and I— Tell me, do you have the feeling you've heard that voice before?"

Conway frowned. "Now that you mention it, I do. There's something in the tempo, in the spacing of the words more than in the tone."

Eva Kane nodded. "We know her," she said. "She's someone who has been in the office. You've talked with her. She's disguising her voice in some way—the tone of it. But the tempo, the way she spaces the words can't be changed. She's someone we both know, and that makes me all the more suspicious. Why should she lie to you? I mean, why should she try to deceive you about her identity?"

"Nevertheless, I'm going to go," Conway announced. "The information is too valuable, too vital. I can't afford to run the chance of passing up a bet of that sort."

Suddenly Eva Kane was back in character, an efficient, impersonal secretary.

"Very well, Mr. Conway," she said, and left the office.

Conway checked his watch with a radio time signal, started his car precisely on the minute, and followed directions. He went through a light just as it was changing and left a car which seemed to be trying to follow him hopelessly snarled in traffic with an irate traffic officer blowing his whistle.

After that, Conway drove in and out of traffic. At five minutes past six he was in the drugstore, waiting in the phone booth farthest from the door.

At six-twelve the phone rang.

Conway answered it.

"Mr. Conway?" a crisply feminine voice asked.

"Yes. . . . Is this—this isn't Rosalind."

"Don't ask questions. Rosalind must take precautions to get rid of the people who were shadowing *her*. Here are your directions. Are you ready?"

"Yes."

"Very well. As soon as you hang up, leave the phone booth and the drugstore. Get in your own car. Drive to the Redfern Hotel. Park your car. Go to the lobby. Tell the clerk that your name is Gerald Boswell and that you're expecting a message. The clerk will hand you an envelope. Thank him, but don't tip him. Walk over to a secluded corner in the lobby and open the envelope. That envelope will give you your cue as to what you're to do next."

She hung up without saying good-by.

Conway left the phone booth, went at once to his car and drove directly to the Redfern Hotel.

"Do you have a message for Gerald Boswell?" he asked the clerk.

For a moment, as the clerk hesitated, Conway was afraid he might be going to ask for some identification, but the hesitation was only momentary. The clerk pulled out a sheaf of envelopes and started going through them.

"Boswell," he said, repeating the name mechanically as he went through the envelopes. "Boswell. What's the first name?"

"Gerald."

"Oh, yes. Gerald Boswell." The clerk handed Conway a long envelope, and for a moment Conway's heart gave a sudden surge. The envelope was of heavy manila, well sealed, well filled. This could be the list of stockholders who had sent in their proxies, the list that would make all the difference in the world to him in his fight to retain the company management.

Conway moved over to a corner of the lobby, sat down in one of the worn, overstuffed chairs as though waiting for someone to join him.

Surreptitiously he sized up the other occupants of the lobby.

There was a middle-aged woman immersed in her newspaper. There was a bored, seedy-looking man who was working a crossword puzzle; a younger woman who seemed to be waiting for someone and who apparently had not the slightest interest in anything other than the street door of the hotel lobby.

Conway slipped his penknife from his pocket, slit open the envelope and slid out the contents.

To his disgust, the envelope contained only pieces of old newspaper which had been cut to a size to fit into the envelope. Nor did these bits of newspaper clippings have any significance or continuity. The sections of newspaper had been cut crosswise and evidently used only to fill out the envelope.

Folded in with these pieces of newspaper, however, was a key attached to an oval brass tag carrying the imprint of the Redfern Hotel and the number of the room, 729.

His sense of prudence urged Conway to terminate the adventure then and there, but the mere thought of so doing gave him a feeling of frustration. The person who had dreamed up this plan had used applied psychology. Once persuaded to do a lot of unconventional things to avoid detection, Conway was conditioned for a step which he would never have considered if it had been put up to him at the start.

Conway pushed the strips of newspaper back into the envelope, put the envelope into the container for wastepaper and moved over toward the elevators. After all, he would at least go up and knock on the door.

The young woman who was operating the elevator seemed completely absorbed in her paperbacked novel. She gave Conway a passing glance, then lowered her eyes.

"Seven," he said.

She moved the cage to the seventh floor, stopped it, let Conway out, and was dropping the cage back to the ground floor before Conway had more than oriented himself as to the sequence of numbers.

The hotel had an aura of second-class semirespectability. The place was clean but it was the cleanliness of sterilization. The carpets were thin. The light fixtures were cheap, and the illumination in the corridor was somewhat dim.

Conway found Room 729 and tapped on the door.

There was no answer.

He waited and tapped again.

The key in his hand was an invitation. The thought of inserting it in the door and entering the room was only a little less distasteful than that of putting the key in his pocket, returning to the elevator and leaving forever unsolved the mystery of the locked room and the possibility of obtaining the lists of stockholders who had sent in proxies.

Jerry Conway fitted the key to the door. The spring lock clicked smoothly, and Conway pushed the door open.

He found himself peering into the conventional sitting room of a two-room hotel suite. The door that he judged would lead to the bedroom was closed.

"Anybody home?" Conway called.

There was no sound.

Conway closed the corridor door behind him, and gave the place a quick inspection. There was hope in his mind that this was part of an elaborate scheme to deliver the papers that he had been promised, a delivery that could be made in such a manner that he would have no contact with the person making the delivery.

He found nothing in the sitting room and was thoughtfully contemplating the bedroom door, when the knob turned and a young woman wearing only a bra, panties and sheer stockings stepped out into the parlor, closing the bedroom door behind her. Apparently, she hadn't even seen Conway. She was humming a little tune.

Her hair was wrapped in a towel. Her face was a dark blob, which Conway soon recognized as a mud pack that extended down to her throat.

The figure was exciting, and the underthings were thin, filmy wisps of black lace which seemed only to emphasize the warm pink of the smooth skin.

Conway stood stock-still, startled and transfixed.

Then abruptly she saw him. For a moment Conway thought she was going to scream. Her mouth opened. The mask of the mud pack kept him from seeing her features. He saw only eyes and the red of a wide-open mouth.

"Now, listen! Let me explain," Conway said, talking rapidly and moving toward the young woman. "I take it you're not Rosalind?"

The figure answered in a thick voice due to the hard mud pack. "I'm Rosalind's roommate, Mildred. Who are you? How did you get in here?"

She might have been twenty-six or twenty-seven, Conway judged. Her figure was full, and every seductive curve was visible.

Standing there in the hotel suite confronting this young woman, Conway had a sense of complete unreality as though he were engaged in some amateur theatrical, playing a part that he didn't fully understand, and confronted by an actress who was trying in an amateurish way to follow directions.

"*How* did you get in?" she demanded in that same thick voice.

"Rosalind gave me her key," Conway said. "I was to meet her here. Now look, Mildred, quit being frightened. I won't hurt you. Go get your clothes on. I'll wait for Rosalind."

"But why should Rosalind have given you a key?" she asked. "I— That isn't at all like Rosalind. . . . You can imagine how *I* feel coming in here half-nude and finding a strange man in the apartment. How do I know Rosalind gave you the key? Who are you, anyway?"

"I've been in touch with Rosalind," Conway said. "She has some papers for me. I was to pick them up here."

"Papers?" Mildred said. "Papers. Let me see." She walked over to the desk with quick, purposeful steps, and again Conway had the feeling that he was watching an actress playing a part.

She pulled back the lid of the desk, put her hand inside,

and suddenly Conway heard the unmistakable click of a double-action revolver being cocked. Then he saw the black, round hole of a barrel held in a trembling hand, the young woman's nervous finger pressing on the trigger.

"Hey!" Conway said. "Don't point that thing at me, you little fool! That may go off!"

"Put your hands up," she said.

"For heaven's sake," Conway told her, "don't be a fool! You've cocked that revolver, and the slightest pressure on the trigger will— Put that gun down! I'm not trying to hurt you!"

She advanced toward him, the revolver now pointing at his middle.

"Get your hands up," she said, her voice taking on an edge of hysteria. "You're going to jail!"

The hand that held the revolver was distinctly trembling, her finger rested against the trigger.

Conway waited while she advanced one more step, measured the distance, suddenly clamped his left hand over her wrist, grasped the gun with his right hand. Her hand was nerveless, and he had no difficulty forcing up the barrel of the revolver and at the same time pushing his thumb over the cocked hammer of the gun.

Conway wrested the gun from her limp grip, carefully lowered the hammer, shoved the weapon in his pocket.

"You little fool!" he said. "You could have killed me! Don't you understand?"

She moved back to the davenport, seated herself, and stared, apparently in abject terror.

Conway stood over her. "Now, listen," he said, "get a grip on yourself. I'm not going to hurt you. I'm not here to make any trouble. I'm only trying to get some papers. from Rosalind. Can't you understand that?"

"Don't hurt me!" she said. "If you'll promise not to kill me, I'll do anything. . . . Don't hurt me! My purse is in

17

the desk. Everything I have is in it. Take it all. Only please don't— Don't . . . !"

"Shut up!" Conway snapped. "I've tried to explain to you! Can't you understand? Can't you listen?"

"Just don't kill me!" she pleaded. "I'll do anything you say if you just won't kill me."

Conway abruptly reached a decision.

"I'm leaving," he said. "Don't go near that telephone for five minutes after I leave. Don't tell anyone that I was here, no one except Rosalind. Do you understand that?"

She simply sat there, her face a wooden mask.

Conway strode to the door, jerked it open, slammed it shut, sprinted down the corridor to the red light that marked the stairwell. He pushed open the door, ran down two flights of stairs to the fifth floor, then hurried over to the elevator and pressed the button.

It seemed an age before the elevator came up, then the door slid open and Conway stepped inside, conscious of his rapid breathing, his pounding heart.

The girl who was operating the elevator shifted her gum to the other side of her face. She held her book in her right hand. Her left hand manipulated the control which dropped the elevator to the ground floor. She didn't even look at his face, but said, "You must have walked down two floors."

Conway, mentally cursing his clumsiness, said nothing. The elevator girl kept her eyes lowered, raising them only for one swift glance.

Conway didn't dare to leave the key to Room 729 on the clerk's desk. Walking when he wanted to run, the revolver in his hip pocket, Conway moved rapidly across the lobby, out of the door of the hotel, and then hurried down the street to the place where he had parked his car.

He jumped inside, started the motor and adjusted himself behind the steering wheel. He became increasingly conscious of the bulge in his hip pocket.

He withdrew the .38-caliber revolver, started to put it in the glove compartment, then just as a matter of precaution, swung open the cylinder.

There were five loaded cartridges in the cylinder, and one empty cartridge case bearing the imprint of the firing pin in the soft percussion cap.

Conway snapped the cylinder back into place, smelled the muzzle of the gun.

The odor of freshly burnt powder clung to the barrel.

In a sudden panic, Conway pushed the gun into the glove compartment, started the car, and drove away from the curb fast.

When he came to a service station where there was a telephone booth, he parked the car and looked up the number of Perry Mason, Attorney at Law.

The directory gave the number of Mason's office. There was no residence phone, but a night number was listed.

Conway called the night number.

A voice came on the line and said, "This is a recorded message. If you are calling the office of Mr. Perry Mason on a matter of major importance, you may call at the office of the Drake Detective Agency, state your name, address, and business, and Mr. Mason will be contacted at the earliest possible moment."

CHAPTER TWO

THE UNLISTED TELEPHONE in Perry Mason's apartment jangled sharply.

Only two persons in the world had that number. One was Della Street, Perry Mason's confidential secretary. The other was Paul Drake, head of the Drake Detective Agency.

Mason, who had been on the point of going out, picked up the receiver.

Paul Drake's voice came over the wire. "Perry! I have a problem that you may want to work on."

"What is it?"

"Have you followed the fight for proxies in the California & Texas Global Development & Exploration Company?"

"I know there is a fight on," Mason said. "I've seen ads in the paper for the last week."

"Jerry Conway, president of the company, is waiting on another telephone. He's calling from a pay station. He's pretty well worked up, thinks he's been framed, and wants to see you at once."

"What kind of frame?" Mason asked. "Some sort of badger game, attempted bribery, or—?"

"He doesn't know," Drake said, "but he has a revolver in his possession and the weapon has been freshly fired. Of course, I've just hit the high spots on the phone with him, but he's got a story that's sufficiently out of the ordinary so you should be interested, and he says he has money enough to pay any fee within reason. He wants action!"

"A revolver!" Mason said.

"That's right."

"How did he get it?"

"He says he took it away from a woman."

"Where?"

"In a hotel room."

"Did he take her there?"

"He says not. He says he had a key to the room, and she came in and pulled this gun on him, that she had a nervous trigger finger, and he took the gun away from her. It wasn't until after he had left the place, that he noticed the gun had been freshly fired and now he's afraid he's being put on the spot."

"That's a hell of a story!" Mason said.

"That's the way it impresses me," Drake told him. "The point is that if the guy is going to be picked up and he's relying on a story as phony as that, somebody should instruct him to at least tell a lie that will sound plausible."

Mason said, "They have to think up their own lies, Paul."

"I know," Paul retorted, "but you could point out where *this* one is full of holes."

"Can he hear your side of this conversation?"

"No."

"Ask him if it's worth a thousand dollars for a retainer," Mason said. "If it is, I'll come up."

"Hold the phone," Drake said. "He's on the other line."

A moment later Drake's voice came back on the wire. "Hello, Perry?"

"Uh-huh," Mason said.

"Conway says it's worth two thousand. He's scared stiff. He thinks he's led with his chin."

"Okay," Mason said. "Tell him to go on up to your office and make out his check for a thousand bucks. Get a couple of good men to stand by in case I need them. I'm on my way up."

Mason switched out the lights in his apartment, and drove to Paul Drake's office.

Jerry Conway jumped up as Mason entered the room.

"I have a feeling that I've walked into a trap, Mr. Mason," he said. "I don't know how bad it is. But . . . well, there's a lot of money involved in this proxy fight, and the people on the other side are willing to do anything. They'll stop at nothing!"

Drake slid a check across the desk to Perry Mason. "I had Conway make out his check for the retainer," he said.

"Got a couple of men lined up?" Mason asked.

Drake nodded.

Mason picked a straight-backed chair, spun it around so that the back was facing the center of the room. He straddled the chair, propped his elbows on the back of the chair and said to Conway, "All right, start talking."

"There isn't much time," Conway said nervously. "Whatever has happened is—"

"There's no use running around blind," Mason said. "You're going to have to take time to tell me the story. Tell it to me fast. Begin at the beginning."

Conway said, "It started with a telephone call."

"Who from?" Mason asked.

"A young woman who gave the name of Rosalind."

"Have you seen her?"

"I don't think so. I don't know."

"Why don't you know?"

"I saw a young woman tonight who said she was Rosalind's roommate. I . . . I'm afraid—"

"Go on," Mason interrupted. "Get it over with! Don't try to make it easy on yourself. Give me the details."

Conway told his story. Mason leaned forward, his arms folded across the back of the chair, his chin resting on his wrists, his eyes narrow with concentration. He asked no questions, took no notes, simply listened with expressionless concentration.

When Conway had finished, Mason said, "Where's the gun?"

Conway took it from his pocket.

Mason didn't touch the gun. "Open the cylinder," he said.

Conway swung open the cylinder.

"Turn it so the light shines on it."

Conway turned the weapon.

"Take out that empty shell," Mason said.

Conway extracted the shell.

Mason leaned forward to smell the barrel and the shell. "All right," he said, still keeping his hands off the gun. "Put it back. Put the gun in your pocket. Where's the key to the room in the hotel?"

"I have it here."

"Pass it over."

Conway handed the key to Perry Mason who inspected it for a moment, then dropped it in his pocket.

Mason turned to Paul Drake. "I'll want you with me, Paul."

"What about me?" Conway asked.

"You stay here."

"What do I do with the gun?"

"Nothing!"

"Shouldn't I notify the police?"

"Not yet."

"Why?"

"Because we don't know what we're up against yet. What about that woman in the room?"

"What about her?"

"Was she really frightened or acting?"

"Her hand was shaking and the gun was wobbling."

23

"When she came out, all she had on were a bra and panties?"

"Yes."

"Good-looking?"

"Her figure was all there."

"Yet she didn't seem embarrassed?"

"She was frightened."

"There's a difference. Was she embarrassed?"

"I . . . I would say just frightened. She didn't try to . . . to cover up."

"How old?"

"Probably late twenties."

"Blond, brunette or redheaded?"

"She had a towel wrapped around her head. All I could see was from the neck down—and I mean all."

"Eyes?"

"I couldn't see well enough to tell."

"Rings?"

"I didn't notice."

"Where did she get the gun?"

"Apparently out of the desk."

"And after that?"

"She acted as though she thought I was going to assault her or something. She wanted to give me all of her money, and begged me not to hurt her."

"Did her voice sound like Rosalind's voice over the telephone?"

"No. This mud pack seemed to have hardened. Her lips couldn't move well. You know how those mud packs act. Her talk was thick—like a person talking while asleep. Rosalind's voice was different.

"I've heard Rosalind's voice before. I have the feeling that I've heard it quite a few times. It wasn't her voice so much as the spacing of the words, the tempo."

"You don't think this girl in the hotel was Rosalind?"

24

"I don't think so."

"You're not sure?"

"I'm not sure of anything."

"Wait here until you hear from me," Mason said. He nodded to the detective. "Let's go, Paul."

Mason crossed the office, held the door open.

"My car or yours?" Drake asked, as they waited for the elevator.

"Mine," Mason said. "It's out here."

"You scare me to death in traffic," Drake told him.

Mason smiled. "No more. When John Talmage was Traffic Editor of the *Deseret News,* he followed all my cases and took me to task for the way I drove. He cited a few statistics."

"Cure you?" Drake asked.

"Made a Christian of me," Mason admitted. "Watch and see."

"I'm skeptical but willing to be convinced," Paul told him.

Mason, carefully complying with all traffic regulations, drove to the Redfern Hotel and found a parking place.

"Going to identify yourself?" Drake asked.

Mason shook his head. "I'll keep in the background. You'll go to the desk, ask if there are any messages for Mr. Boswell."

Drake raised his eyebrows.

"In that way," Mason said, "we'll find out if the clerk remembers Conway coming in and asking the same question. If he does, he'll look at you suspiciously and start asking questions. Then you can identify yourself and we'll start from there."

"And if he doesn't remember?" Drake asked.

"Then," Mason said, "you talk with him long enough for him to remember your face. Then if anyone asks him to identify the person who came to the desk and inquired for messages for Boswell, he'll be confused on the identification."

"Suppose there's a Boswell registered in the hotel. Then what do we do?"

"We first go to the room phones, say we want to speak with Gerald Boswell. Find out if he's registered. If he isn't, we go up to 729 and look around."

"For what?"

"Perhaps we'll find the girl under that mud pack."

The two men entered the Redfern Hotel and went to the house phones. Mason first asked for Gerald Boswell and was told he was in Room 729. There was no answer.

"Go on, Paul," Mason said, handing him the key.

Paul Drake walked to the desk, stood there quietly.

The clerk looked up from some bookkeeping he was doing, came over to the counter.

"Messages for Boswell?" Drake asked.

"What's the first name?"

"Gerald."

The clerk moved over to the pigeonholes, picked out a stack of envelopes from the one marked "B," and started flipping them over.

Abruptly he stopped, looked up at Paul Drake, said, "You were in here earlier, weren't you, Mr. Boswell? Didn't I give you an envelope?"

Drake grinned. "Let's put it this way: I'm looking for a *recent* message."

"I'm quite certain there isn't any," the clerk said. "I gave you that— Or was it you?"

Drake said casually, "That envelope. What's come in since?"

"Nothing!"

"You're certain?"

"Yes."

"Look it over again and make certain."

The clerk looked through the file, then regarded Drake dubiously. "I beg your pardon, Mr. Boswell, but do you have any means of identification?"

"Sure," Drake said.

"May I see it?"

Drake took the key to 729 from his pocket and tossed it on the counter in front of the clerk.

"729," the clerk said.

"Right," Drake said.

The clerk moved over to the directory of guests, looked under 729, then became apologetic. "I'm sorry, Mr. Boswell. I was just making certain, that's all. If any recent messages came in, they would be in the key box. There's nothing. . . . You didn't have anyone else come in this evening and ask for messages, did you?"

"Me?" Drake asked in surprise.

The clerk nodded.

"Don't be silly," Drake told him. "I'm able to get around. I take my own messages."

"And I gave you a letter earlier?"

"There was a message in a brown manila envelope," Drake said.

The clerk's face showed relief. "I was afraid for a minute that I'd given it to the wrong party. Thank you very much."

"Not at all," Drake said and, picking up his key, moved over to the elevator.

Mason moved over to join him.

The girl in the elevator was reading her paperbacked novel. The picture on the cover depicted a good-looking woman in panties and bra, engaged in casual conversation with a man in evening clothes. The title was *No Smog Tomorrow.*

The elevator girl didn't look up. As Mason and Drake entered, and as the cage moved under their added weight, the

27

operator closed the book, holding her forefinger to mark the page.

"Floor?" she asked.

"Seven," Drake said.

She started chewing gum as though the book had been sufficiently absorbing to make her forget about the gum.

"What's your book?" Drake asked.

"A novel," she said shortly, looking up for the first time.

"Looks spicy," Drake said.

"Any law against my reading what I want?"

"None," Drake said.

"You can buy it yourself at the newsstand for twenty-five cents, in case you're interested."

"I'm interested," Drake told her.

She flashed him a quick glance.

"But not twenty-five cents' worth," the detective added.

She diverted her eyes, pouted, jerked the cage to a stop, said, "Seventh floor."

Mason and Paul Drake walked out and down the corridor.

The girl held the cage at the seventh floor. The mirror on the side of the elevator shaft showed her eyes as she watched the two men walking down the corridor.

"Go right to 729?" Drake asked Mason in a low voice. "She's watching."

"Sure," Mason said.

"She's interested."

"So much the better."

Mason paused before the door of 729. He knocked twice. There was no answer.

Drake produced the key, glanced at Mason.

The lawyer nodded. Drake inserted the key, clicked back the latch.

The door swung back on well-oiled hinges.

There was no one in the room, although the lights were on.

Mason entered the room, closed the door behind him, called, "Anyone there?"

No one answered.

Mason walked to the partially opened door leading into the bedroom. He knocked gently.

"Everybody decent?" he called, waited for a moment for an answer, then pushed open the door.

Abruptly he recoiled.

"All right, Paul, we've found it!"

Drake came to stand at Mason's side. The body of the girl was sprawled diagonally across one of the twin beds. Her left arm and the head were over the far edge of the bed, blond hair hung straight down alongside the dangling arm. The girl wore a tight-fitting, light-blue sweater, and blood from a bullet wound in the left side of the chest had turned the sweater to a purplish hue. The right arm was raised as though to ward off a blow at her face, and remained stiffly grotesque. The short, disarranged skirt disclosed neat nylon legs doubled up and crossed at the ankles.

Mason crossed to the body, felt the wrist, and put slight pressure on the upturned right arm.

Puzzled, he moved around to the side of the bed and touched the left arm.

The left arm swung limply from the shoulder.

Paul Drake said, "Good Lord, Perry, we're in a jam. We've *got* to report this. I insist."

Mason, regarding the body in frowning concentration, said, "Okay, Paul, we'll report it."

Drake lunged for the telephone in the room.

"Not here! Not now!" Mason said sharply.

"We have to," Drake said. "Otherwise we'll be concealing evidence and making ourselves accessories. We've got to turn Conway in and let him—"

29

"What do you mean, we have to turn Conway in?" Mason interrupted. "Conway is my client."

"But he's mixed up in this thing!"

"How do you know he is?"

"He admits it!"

"The hell he does. As far as we know, there was no body in the room when he left. This isn't the girl *he* left here. If it is, she dressed after he left."

"What do you intend to do?" Drake asked.

"Come on," Mason told him.

"Look, Perry, I've got a license. They can take it away. They—"

"Forget it," Mason said. "I'm running the show. You're acting under my instructions. I'm taking the responsibility. Come on!"

"Where?"

"To the nearest phone booth where we can have privacy. First, however, we give it a quick once-over."

"No, Perry, no. We can't touch anything. You know that."

"We can look around," Mason said. "Bathroom door partially open. No sign of baggage, no clothes anywhere. Conway said the girl was in undies and was supposed to be Rosalind's roommate. This place doesn't look lived in."

"Come on, Perry, for the love of Mike," Drake protested. "It's a trap. If they catch us prowling the place, we'll be the ones in the trap. We can claim we were going to phone in a report and they'll laugh at us, want to know what we were doing prowling the joint."

Mason opened a closet door. "I shouldn't have brought you along, Paul."

"You can say that again," Drake said.

Mason regarded the empty closet.

"Okay, Paul, let's go to the lobby and phone. This is a trap, all right. Let's go."

Drake followed the lawyer to the elevator. The elevator girl had brought the cage back to the seventh floor. She was sitting on the stool, her knees crossed, good-looking legs where they could be seen.

She was looking at the book but seemed more interested in her pose than in the book.

She looked up as Mason and Paul Drake entered the elevator. She closed the book, marking the place with her right forefinger. Her eyes rested on Paul Drake.

"Down?" she asked.

"Down," Mason said.

She looked Paul Drake over as she dropped the cage to the ground floor.

Drake, engrossed in his thoughts, didn't give her so much as a glance.

Mason crossed the lobby to a telephone booth, dropped a dime, and dialed the unlisted number of Della Street, his confidential secretary.

Della Street's voice said, "Hello."

"You decent?" Mason asked.

"Reasonably."

"Okay. Jump in your car. Go to Paul Drake's office. You'll find a man there. His name's Conway. Identify yourself. Tell him I said he was to go with you. Get him out of circulation."

"Where?"

Mason said, "Put him anyplace, just so it isn't the Redfern Hotel."

Della Street's voice was sharp with concentration. "Anything else?"

"Be sure that he registers under his right name," Mason said. "Got that?"

"Yes, Chief."

"All right. Listen carefully. He heard a woman's voice on the telephone. There was something in the spacing of that voice he thinks was familiar. The voice itself was disguised, but there was something in the tempo he's heard before.

"Now, it's important as hell that he identify that voice. Keep after him. Make him think. Hold his nose to the grindstone. Tell him I have to have the answer."

"What shall I tell him about the reason for all this?" Della asked.

"Tell him you're following my instructions. *Make* him remember what it is about that voice that's familiar."

"Okay. That all?"

"That's all. Get started. You haven't much time. Return to the office after you get him located. Be discreet. Act fast."

"Where are you now?"

"At the Redfern Hotel."

"Can I reach you there?"

"No. Don't try to reach me anywhere. Get this man out of circulation, then go to the office and wait."

"Okay, Chief, I'm on my way."

Mason hung up, dropped another dime, dialed police headquarters and said, "Homicide, please."

A moment later, when he had Homicide on the line, he said, "This is Perry Mason, the attorney."

"Just a minute," the man's voice said. "Sgt. Holcomb's here. I'll put him on."

"Oh-oh," Mason said.

Sgt. Holcomb's voice came over the line. "Yes, Mr. Mason," he said with overdone politeness. "What can we do for you tonight?"

"For one thing," Mason said, "you can go to the Redfern Hotel, Room 729, and look at the body of a young woman who's sprawled across one of the twin beds in the bedroom. I've been careful not to touch anything, but it's my opinion that she's quite dead."

"Where are you now?" Holcomb asked sharply.

"In the telephone booth in the lobby of the Redfern Hotel."

"You've been up in the room?"

"Naturally," Mason said. "I'm not psychic. When I tell you a body's there, it means I've seen it."

"Why didn't you use the room phone?"

"Didn't want to foul up any fingerprints," Mason said. "We came down here and used the phone in the lobby."

"Have you told anyone about this?"

"I've told you."

Holcomb said, "I'll have a radio car there in two minutes. I'll be there myself in fifteen minutes."

"We'll wait for you," Mason said. "The room's locked."

"How did you get in?"

"I had a key."

"The hell you did!"

"That's right."

"Whose room is it?"

"The room is registered in the name of Gerald Boswell."

"You know him?"

"As far as I know," Mason said, "I've never seen him in my life."

"Then how did you have the key?"

"It was given to me."

"You wait right there," Holcomb said.

Mason hung up the phone, said to Paul Drake, "Well, we may as well wait."

The lawyer seated himself in one of the overstuffed, leather chairs.

Drake, after a moment, eased himself into an adjoining chair. He was obviously unhappy.

The clerk behind the desk eyed them thoughtfully.

Mason took a cigarette case from his pocket, extracted a

cigarette, tapped the end, held flame to the end of the cigarette and inhaled a deep drag.

"What the devil am I going to tell them?" Drake asked.

"I'll do the talking," Mason told him.

They had waited less than a minute when the door opened, and a uniformed police officer hurried in. He went to the desk, talked briefly to the clerk.

The startled clerk pointed to Mason and Paul Drake. The officer came over to them.

"Are you the men who reported a body?" he asked.

"That's right," Mason told him.

"Where is it?"

"Room 729," Mason said. "Do you want a key?"

The lawyer took the room key from his pocket, and handed it to the officer.

"Homicide says for you to wait here. I'm to seal up the room until they can get here."

"Okay," Mason told him. "We're waiting."

"You're Perry Mason?"

"That's right."

"Who's this?"

"Paul Drake, private detective."

"How'd you happen to discover the body?"

"We opened the door and walked in," Mason said. And then added, "Are you supposed to get our story now, or get up and see no one is in the room tampering with evidence?"

The officer said curtly, "Don't go away!" He grabbed the key and hurried to the elevator.

The excited clerk was conferring with the girl at the hotel switchboard. A moment later she started making frantic calls.

Mason pinched out his cigarette in an ash tray.

"They'll make us tell the whole story," Drake said.

"Everything we *know*," Mason said. "We're not supposed

to do any guessing for the police, only give them the evidence we have."

"And the name of our client?"

"Not *our* client," Mason said sharply. "*My* client. He's nothing to you. *I'm* your client."

Mason walked over to the hotel desk, took an envelope from the rack, addressed it to himself at his office, put a stamp on the envelope, moved over to the mailbox.

Drake came to stand beside him.

Mason took Conway's check for a thousand dollars from his pocket, pushed it in the envelope, sealed the envelope, and dropped it in the mailbox.

"What's that for?" Drake asked.

"Someone might book me for something and search me," Mason said. "Even Sgt. Holcomb would connect up a thousand-dollar retainer with our visit to the Redfern Hotel."

"I don't like this," Drake said.

"Who does?" Mason asked.

"Are we in the clear withholding Conway's name?"

"Why not? Conway didn't commit any murder."

"How do you know he didn't?"

"He says he didn't."

"He has the gun."

"What gun?"

"The one with which the murder was committed!"

"How do you know it's the gun?" Mason asked.

"It has to be," Drake said.

"I told you," Mason told him, "we're not supposed to engage in any surmises or jump to any conclusions as far as the police are concerned. We're supposed to tell them what we know, provided it isn't a privileged communication."

Drake said, "They'll sweat it out of us."

"Not out of me, they won't," Mason told him.

"They'll find Conway in my office."

Mason shook his head.

"So that's it!" Drake said. "That was the first telephone call you made!"

Mason yawned, reached for his cigarette case, said, "You're not supposed to deal in surmises when you're talking with the police, Paul, only facts. That's all they're interested in."

Drake cracked his knuckles nervously.

The clerk left the desk and came over to join them. "Did you two report a body in 729?" he asked.

"Sure," Mason said, as though surprised at the question.

"How did it happen you did that?"

"Because we found a body," Mason told him. "You're supposed to report to the police on things like that."

"I mean, how did you happen to find the body?"

"Because she was there."

"Dead or passed out?" the clerk asked.

"She looked dead, but I'm not a doctor."

"Mr. Boswell was with you when you found the body?" the clerk asked.

"Boswell?" Mason asked in surprise.

The clerk nodded toward Paul Drake.

"That's not Boswell," Mason said.

"He claimed he was Boswell," the clerk said accusingly.

"No, he didn't," Mason said. "He asked if there were any messages for Mr. Boswell."

"And I asked him to identify himself," the clerk said indignantly.

"And he put the key to 729 on the counter," Mason said. "You went and looked up the registration and found it was in the name of Boswell. You felt that was all the identification you needed. You didn't ask him for a driving license. You didn't ask him if his name was Boswell. You asked him for identification, and he put the key on the counter."

The clerk said indignantly, "I was led to believe I was

dealing with Mr. Boswell. The police aren't going to like this."

"That's unfortunate," Mason said, and then added, "for you."

"I asked him for identification as Boswell."

"No you didn't. You asked him for *some* identification."

"That's a technicality, and you know it."

"What's a technicality?"

"I meant that I wanted to know who he was. I wanted to see his identification."

"Then you should have asked him for it and insisted on seeing it," Mason said. "Don't try to hold *us* responsible for *your* mistakes."

"The room is registered in the name of Gerald Boswell."

"Uh-huh," Mason said.

"And this is the man who claimed to be Boswell earlier in the evening. He got an envelope from me."

"You're sure?" Mason asked.

"Of course I'm sure."

"You weren't so sure a moment ago."

"I *was* sure."

"Then why did you ask him for identification?"

"I wanted to be certain he was the same man."

"Then you *weren't* certain."

"I'm not going to let you cross-examine me."

"That's what you think," Mason told him, grinning. "Before you get done, you'll be on the witness stand. Then I'll give you a *real* cross-examination."

"Who are you?"

"The name's Perry Mason."

The clerk was nonplused. "The lawyer?"

"That's right."

Abruptly the door of the lobby pushed open, and Sgt. Holcomb, followed by two officers in plain clothes, came striding across toward the elevators, saw Mason, Drake and the clerk, and detoured over to them.

"Good evening, Sergeant," Mason said cordially.

Sgt. Holcomb ignored the greeting.

He glared at Perry Mason. "How does it happen *you're* in on this?"

"In the interests of my client, I went to 729 to look for some evidence," Mason said.

"In the interests of whom?"

"A client."

"All right," Holcomb said, "let's quit playing ring-around-the-rosy. This is murder. Who was the client?"

Mason shook his head and said, "That information is confidential."

"You can't withhold that," Holcomb told him. "You'll become an accessory, if you try to protect a murderer."

"This man wasn't a murderer," Mason said.

"How do you know?"

"I know. Furthermore, he's my client. I don't have to divulge the names of my clients to anyone."

"You can't withhold evidence."

"I'm not withholding any *evidence*. As soon as I entered the room, I found a body. As soon as I found the body, I notified you."

The clerk said, "Excuse me, Sergeant, but this man standing here is the client."

Sgt. Holcomb said disdainfully, "Don't be silly. That guy's the private detective who does Mason's investigative work. Mason called him in after he knew there'd been a murder."

"I'm sorry, Sergeant," the clerk protested, "but that isn't true in this case."

"How do you know?"

"That's the man who got the key to the room in the first

38

place. His secretary registered for him. He's been in several times asking for messages."

Sgt. Holcomb turned to Paul Drake. "Hey! Wait a minute! Wait a minute! What's all this?"

Paul Drake said, "The guy's nuts!"

"What's your name?" Holcomb asked the clerk.

"Bob King."

"All right. Now, what's this about the room?"

"It was rented about two o'clock. A young woman came to the desk and said she was the secretary of Gerald Boswell, that Boswell wanted to have a suite in the hotel for one day, that he would appear later, and go to the suite, but that she wanted to inspect it and make sure it was okay, that since she had no baggage, she would pay the rent in advance and take the keys. She asked for two keys."

"Say," Holcomb said, "you're giving out a hell of a lot of valuable information."

"Well, you asked for it. What's valuable about it?"

Holcomb jerked his head toward Mason. "He's drinking it in."

"Well, you asked me."

"All right. Now shut up. . . . Wait a minute. Tell me about Paul Drake here."

"He showed up about six-thirty, asked for a message, gave the name of Boswell, and I went through the file and gave him an envelope."

"An envelope containing a key?" Holcomb asked.

"Perhaps the key was in it, but as I remember it now, and it's beginning to come back to me, it was a big, heavy manila envelope, thick, and jammed with papers."

"And it was Paul Drake here who got the letter?"

"I think so. . . . Yes, this was the man."

"Then what did he do?"

"Went up to the suite. I didn't pay much attention. He

seemed quiet and respectable, and the suite was paid for in advance."

Holcomb whirled to Paul Drake and said, "What about this?"

Drake hesitated.

"I can answer for Paul Drake," Mason said. "I think there has been a case of mistaken identity."

"The hell there has!" Sgt. Holcomb said. "Drake went up there on some kind of job for you! This girl got herself bumped off in his room, and he sent out an SOS for you. He didn't stay in the suite, did he?" Holcomb asked the clerk.

"I don't know. I didn't pay attention. He came back this second time and asked for messages. That was when I had occasion to look at him particularly, because these two gentlemen were together and I asked this man, who you say is Mr. Drake but who gave me the name of Boswell, if I hadn't already given him a message."

Sgt. Holcomb said to Drake, "We may not be able to make Mason kick through with the name of a client, but we can sure as hell make a private detective tell what he knows about a murder or bust him wide open."

Mason said, "I tell you, Sergeant, it's a case of mistaken identification."

"Phooey!" Holcomb said. "I'm going up and take a look at the place. We'll have a fingerprint man up there. If we find your prints and—"

"We were up there," Mason said. "No one questions that. That's where we discovered the body."

"Drake with you?"

"Yes."

"You came in together?"

"That's right."

"What about the story King tells about Drake going to the desk and asking for messages?"

"That part of it is true," Mason said. "We had reason to believe the suite was registered in the name of Boswell, and Drake, acting purely in an investigative capacity, asked if there were any messages for Boswell. He never said he was Boswell."

Sgt. Holcomb said, "This thing sounds fishy as hell to me. You two stick around. I'm going up. Remember now, don't leave. I want to question you further."

Holcomb strode toward the elevator.

Mason turned to Paul Drake, said, "Get on the phone, Paul. Start locating more operatives. I want half a dozen men and a couple of good-looking women, if I can get them."

"You can get them," Drake said, "but, if you don't mind my asking the question, just what the hell do you intend to do?"

"Protect my client, of course," Mason told him.

"I mean about me," Drake said.

"I'm going to get you off the hook," Mason told him.

"How?"

"By letting you tell everything you know."

"But I know the name of your client."

"I can't keep him out of it," Mason said. "He's walked into a trap. All I can hope to do now is to gain time."

"How much time?"

"A few hours."

"What can you do in that time?" Drake asked.

"I don't know until I try," Mason said. "Get on the phone and line up some good operatives. Have them at your office. Come on, Paul. Let's go!"

Drake went to the telephone booth.

Mason lit a cigarette, paced the floor of the lobby thoughtfully.

A deputy coroner, carrying a black bag, two plain-clothes

men, and a police photographer loaded with cameras and flashbulbs entered the hotel.

Sgt. Holcomb came back down as Drake finished with his telephoning.

"All right," Holcomb said. "What do you know about this?"

"Only what we've told you," Mason said. "We went to that room. We entered it. We found a corpse. We called you."

"I know, I know," Holcomb said. "But how did you happen to go to that room in the first place?"

"I was acting on behalf of a client."

"All right. Who's the client?"

"I can't tell you the name of my client until I get his permission."

"Then get his permission."

"I will, but I can't get it now. I'll get it first thing in the morning."

"Well, you can't hold out on us in a case like this. It's one thing being an attorney, and another thing to be an accessory."

"I'm not trying to hold out," Mason said. "I can't betray the confidences of my client. My client will have to speak for himself. I need time to get in touch with him."

"Tell me who he is and *we'll* let him speak for himself."

Mason shook his head. "I can't give you his name without his permission. I'll have my client at the district attorney's office at nine o'clock in the morning. My client will submit to questioning. I'll be there. I'll advise him as to his rights. I can tell you this, Sergeant: To the best of my client's knowledge, there was no corpse in the suite when my client left it. I expected to meet someone there."

"Who?"

"A woman."

"This one who was killed?"

"I don't think so."

"Look, we want to talk with this guy, whoever he is."

"At nine in the morning," Mason said firmly.

Holcomb regarded him with smoldering hostility. "I *could* take *you* in as a material witness."

"To what?" Mason asked. "I've told you all I know about the murder. As far as the private affairs of my client are concerned, he's going to speak for himself. Now, if you want to start getting tough, we'll both get tough and I'll withdraw my offer to have my client at the D.A.'s office at nine in the morning."

Holcomb said angrily, "All right, have it your way. But remember this. We're not considering this as co-operation. You have your client there at nine o'clock, and he won't be entitled to one damned bit of consideration."

"He'll be there," Mason said, "and we're not asking for consideration. We're asking for our rights. And I think I know what they are. . . . Come on, Paul."

Mason turned and walked out.

CHAPTER THREE

IT WAS SHORTLY AFTER eight-thirty that evening when Mason and Drake left the elevator and walked down the echoing corridor of the office building.

The lawyer left Drake at the lighted door in the office of the Drake Detective Agency and kept on down the corridor. He turned at a right angle, walked to the door marked PERRY MASON, ATTORNEY AT LAW, PRIVATE, fitted his latchkey and opened the door.

Della Street was seated at her secretarial desk reading a newspaper.

She dropped the paper to the floor, ran toward Mason almost by the time he had the door open.

"Chief," she said, "what is it? Is it . . . a murder?"

Mason nodded.

"Who found the body?"

"We did."

"That's bad!"

"I know," Mason said, putting his arm around her shoulder and patting her reassuringly. "We always seem to be finding bodies."

"Who was it?"

"No one seems to know. Rather an attractive young woman sprawled out on a bed. What about our client?"

"He's taken care of."

"Where?"

"Do you remember the Gladedell Motel?"

Mason nodded.

"The man who runs it is friendly, and it's close in."

Mason nodded.

"Did you call on the manager personally?"

She shook her head. "We drove down together. I had Mr. Conway let me out a block and a half from the motel. Then he went in and registered by himself, came back, picked me up, reported and took me to where I could get a taxicab. He's in Unit 21. I came back by cab. I didn't want to use my own car. I was afraid someone might notice the license number if I left it parked near the motel."

"How much did you find out on the trip down?" Mason asked.

"Quite a bit."

"Such as?"

"Jerry Conway's a very eligible bachelor. He seems to be

really a grand person. He takes an interest in the people who work with him and seems to be on the up and up.

"Giff Farrell worked for Conway for a year or two, then Conway helped him get promoted to assistant manager. It took Conway a year to find it out, but Farrell was systematically trying to undermine Conway. He started rumors. He got confidential information from the files and used it in such a way that it would make things more difficult for Conway. In fact, he did everything he could to get Conway in bad. Finally Conway found out about it and fired him. Farrell took the matter to the directors and he had been preparing his case for months. He'd made careful note of all sorts of things that had happened, and I guess there was quite a scene at the directors' meeting."

Mason nodded.

"Farrell almost made it stick. He might have done so, if it hadn't been for the loyalty of one of the secretaries. Conway was able to show that Farrell had been passing confidential information on to a competitive company, simply in order to discredit the program Conway was carrying out. When that became apparent, the directors threw Farrell out. Farrell waited for an opportunity and then started this campaign trying to get proxies.

"Now then," she went on, "I worked on him all the way down to see if he could place the voice of the person who phoned him. He seems to think the voice was disguised as to tone, and it was the tempo that was hauntingly familiar. He just can't place it.

"I told him to keep working on it and phone Drake's office if he came up with any answers.

"His secretary, Eva Kane, used to be a phone operator and is accustomed to listening to voices on the phone. She feels positive the voice was that of someone they both know."

Mason said, "Well, I've got to go talk with Conway. You'd better go home, Della."

She smiled and shook her head. "I'll stay and hold the fort for a while. Phone if you want anything. I'll make some coffee in the electric percolator."

Mason drove his car past the lighted office of the Glade-dell Motel, stopped in front of Unit 21, parking his car beside Conway's car, and switched out the lights.

Jerry Conway opened the door of Unit 21, but didn't come out in the light. He stood back on the inside and said, "Come on in, Mason."

Mason entered and closed the door behind him.

Conway indicated a chair for Mason, seated himself on the edge of the bed.

"How bad is it?" he asked.

Mason said, "Keep your voice down. These units are close together, and the walls may be thin. It's bad!"

"How bad?"

"Murder!"

"Murder!" Conway exclaimed.

"Watch it!" Mason warned. "Keep your voice down."

"Good heavens!"

"You should have known," Mason told him. "I wouldn't have spirited you down here unless it had been serious."

"I knew it was bad . . . but I hadn't— Who was killed? Farrell?"

"No, some woman."

"A woman?"

"That's right, a young woman. Now, tell me if you've seen her, and I want you to think it over carefully. This is a woman about twenty-six or twenty-seven, blond, with blue eyes and a good figure, but perhaps a little overdeveloped. The waist seemed slim, but she had curves above and below. She was wearing a light-blue sweater that probably matched her eyes."

Conway thought for a moment, then shook his head. "She means nothing to me—unless she was the girl I saw. She had black-lace underthings. I think her eyes were sort of light, but that black mud pack on her face would make her eyes seem light. I can remember how the whites of the eyes glistened."

"How about young women you know?" Mason asked. "Any of them fit that description?"

"Listen," Conway said impatiently, "we have fifteen or twenty girls working for us. I can't seem to place one of that description offhand. You say she's good-looking?"

"Very!"

Conway thought again, shook his head.

"Try tying it up with the voice?" Mason asked.

"I've been trying to."

"Let's take a look at that gun."

Conway handed Mason the revolver. Mason broke it open, looked at it, took down the numbers in his notebook.

"You're going to try to trace it?" Conway asked.

"That's right," Mason said. "C 48809. I'll try to trace it. What about this secretary of yours? Where does she live?"

"Eva Kane. Cloudcroft Apartments."

Mason said, "You're going to have to go before the D.A. tomorrow morning at nine o'clock and tell your story."

"Do I have to?"

Mason nodded.

"What do I tell him?"

"I'll be with you," Mason said. "I'll pick you up at eight o'clock. We'll talk on the way in."

"Here?"

"Here," Mason said.

"How about going back to my apartment?"

Mason shook his head.

"Why not?" Conway asked. "They won't be able to get a

line on me this early. I want to get some things: tooth brush, pajamas, razor, and a clean shirt."

Mason said, "Go to an all-night drugstore. Buy shaving things and toothbrush. You'll have to get along without the clean shirt."

"Surely you don't think they'd spot me if I went to my apartment?"

"Why not?" Mason asked. "Someone set a trap for you. We don't know when that someone intends to spring the trap. Perhaps he'd like to have you sit tight for four or five days before giving a tip-off to the police and having you picked up. By that time, your silence would have made it seem all the worse. On the other hand, perhaps he knows that I'm in the picture and has decided to tip off the police so they can pick you up before I'll have a chance to find out what it's all about and advise you what to do."

"Well, *you* can't do anything between now and nine o'clock tomorrow morning," Conway said.

"The hell I can't!" Mason told him. "I'm going to have a busy night. You go to an all-night drugstore, get what you want, then come back here and stay here."

"Do I keep the gun?"

"You keep it!" Mason said. "And be damned sure that nothing happens to it!"

"Why? Oh yes, I see your point. If I should try to get rid of it, that would be playing right into their hands."

"Right into their hands is right," Mason said. "It would amount to an acknowledgment of guilt. I want you to tell your story, tell it in your way up to the time you left the hotel, got in your car and drove away."

"I stop there?"

"You stop there," Mason said. "Don't tell them where you spent the night or anything about it. It's none of their damned business. I told the police I'd have you at the D.A.'s office at nine o'clock in the morning, and you're going to be there."

"You know what this means?" Conway said. "Unless I can convince the police, it's going to put me behind the eight ball. If the police should detain me or accuse me of having fired the fatal shot, you can realize what would happen at that stockholders' meeting!"

"Sure!" Mason said. "Why do you suppose a trap was set for you in the first place?"

"Somehow," Conway said, "I can't believe that it was a trap."

"You can't believe it was a trap!" Mason exclaimed. "Hell's bells! The thing sticks out like a sore thumb. Here was this girl in her undies pulling a gun on you, her hand shaking, and she walked toward you, *kept walking toward you!*"

"Well, what's wrong with that?"

"Everything!" Mason said. "A girl half-nude getting a gun out of the desk would have been backing away from you and telling you to get out of the room. She didn't tell you to get out of the room. She told you to put your hands up and she kept walking toward you with the gun cocked and her hand shaking. You just *had* to take it away from her. She did everything but shove it in your hand."

"You think it will turn out to be the murder weapon?"

"I know damned well it will be the murder weapon!" Mason said. "And you'll probably find that the young woman who was murdered was someone who had this list of stockholders who had sent in their proxies."

Conway thought that over for a moment. "Yes, that part of it was a trap, all right. It had to be a trap. Yet somehow, Mason, I have the distinct feeling that there was an element of sincerity about that woman who called herself Rosalind. I think if we can ever get to the bottom of it, we'll find that—I wonder if that young woman who was killed was Rosalind."

"Chances are about ten to one that she was. This girl told you that she was Rosalind's roommate, and that was their suite. That suite has been stripped clean. There isn't so much as a pair of stockings in the place, no clothes, no baggage, nothing."

"But won't that make it look all the more like a trap? Can't we explain to the D.A. that I was framed?"

"Sure we can," Mason said. "Then we can try to make it stick. A good deal depends on whether we can find something to back up your story. The way you tell it, it sounds fishy as hell!"

"But I'm telling the truth," Conway said.

"I know," Mason told him, "but the D.A. is going to be cold, hostile, and bitter. He won't like it because you didn't go to the police instead of consulting an attorney. What's more, we don't know yet how much of a trap you've walked into."

"You think there's more?"

"Sure, there's more," Mason said. "But there are some things about it I can't figure."

"Such as what?"

"If the idea had been to frame you for murder," Mason told him, "they'd have gone about it in a different way. If the Farrell crowd had been willing to take a chance on a killing, it would have been easier for them to have killed you and let it go at that.

"The evidence seems to indicate that they'd been planting one kind of trap for you to walk into, and then something happened and they found themselves with a corpse on their hands. So then they worked fast and tried to switch things around so they had you on a murder rap. When they start moving fast like that, they can easily make mistakes.

If they make just one mistake, we may be able to trip them."

Conway said, "I know that I look like a fool in this thing, Mason, but hang it! I can't get over feeling that this Rosalind was sincere, that she really had this information she wanted to give me, that she was in danger. She said herself that she might be killed if anyone thought she was going to turn over this information to me."

"That makes sense," Mason told him. "If she wasn't tied up with Farrell in *some* way, she wouldn't have had access to the information you wanted. If she *was* tied up with Farrell and was going to run out on him, almost anything could have happened."

Suddenly Conway's face lit up. He snapped his fingers.

"What?" Mason asked.

"I'm just getting an idea," Conway said. "Why should I have to wait here like a sitting duck while *they* start sniping at *me?* Why couldn't I double-cross them at this stage of the game?"

"How?" Mason asked.

"Let me think. I may have an idea."

"Ideas are all right," Mason told him, "but let's be damned certain that you don't do anything that backfires. So far you've had things done to you. Let's keep it that way."

Conway thought for a moment, then said, "Hang it, Mason! Farrell is mixed up in this thing. He had to be the one who killed that girl. He—"

"Now, wait a minute," Mason said. "Don't start trying to think out antidotes until we're sure what the poison is and how much of a dose you've had."

Conway was excited now. "I tell you I'm certain. This girl Rosalind was sincere. She was terrified. She told me herself that she was afraid she'd be killed if anyone knew. . . . Farrell found out what she was doing and—"

"And you think Farrell killed her?"

"No," Conway said, "but I think this Gashouse Baker, or some of his thugs did, and then Farrell got in a panic and tried to blame it on me."

"That checks," Mason said. "I'm willing to ride along with you on that, but so far it's just an idea."

"Farrell tried to trap me," Conway said. "I—"

Abruptly he broke off.

"Well?" Mason asked.

"Let me think," Conway told him.

"All right. Do your thinking," Mason said, "but don't start moving until you know where you are. In the meantime, ring up your secretary and tell her that I'm coming up to talk with her."

"Shall I tell her anything about what happened?"

"Don't tell her what happened. Don't tell her where you are," Mason said. "Simply tell her that I'm coming up to talk with her, that I'm your attorney, that you want her to co-operate with me to the limit. Tell her nothing else."

"Okay," Conway said. "I'd better get busy. I've got a lot of things to do."

Mason looked at him suspiciously. "Such as what?"

"Such as getting that phone call through, getting to an all-night drugstore and making my purchases."

Mason regarded him thoughtfully. "You're getting filled with energy all at once."

"When there's something to be done, I want to get started."

"All right," Mason said, "start in by calling your secretary. Tell her I'll be there in fifteen minutes."

"And I'll see you at eight o'clock in the morning?"

"A little after eight," Mason said. "Be sure you have breakfast. You won't want to tackle what we're going up against on an empty stomach."

CHAPTER FOUR

Mason LEFT THE MOTEL, stopped at a phone booth, called Paul Drake's office.

"Anyone found out who the corpse is, Paul?"

"Not yet."

"I've got a job for you."

"What?"

"I want that gun traced."

"What's the number?"

"Smith & Wesson C 48809."

"It won't be easy to get the dope on it tonight."

"I didn't ask you if it would be easy. I said I wanted it traced."

"Have a heart, Perry!"

"I'm having a heart. I told you to get your men lined up. Now put 'em to work."

"Will I be seeing you?"

"In an hour or two."

Mason hung up the phone, drove to the Cloudcroft Apartments, and tapped gently on the door of Eva Kane's apartment.

The door was almost instantly opened.

"Miss Kane?"

"Yes. Mr. Mason?"

"That's right."

"Come in, please. Mr. Conway telephoned about you."

Mason entered a typical one-room furnished apartment, wide-mirrored doors concealing the roll-away bed. Here and there were bits of individual touches, but for the most part the apartment adhered to the standard pattern.

"Do sit down, Mr. Mason. That chair is fairly comfortable. Can you tell me what happened?"

"What do you mean, what happened?" Mason asked.

"You see, the last I knew Mr. Conway was going out to keep that appointment. I begged him not to. I had a premonition that something terrible was going to happen."

"It's all right," Mason said. "We're in the middle of a three-ring circus, and I'd like to start getting things unscrambled before too many people catch up with me."

"But what happened? Is Mr. Conway—? He told me he was not in his apartment, and he couldn't tell me where he was."

"He's temporarily out of circulation," Mason said. "We're going to be at the district attorney's office at nine o'clock in the morning."

"The district attorney's office!"

Mason nodded.

"Why?"

"Someone got killed."

"Killed!"

Mason nodded. "Murdered."

"Who was it?"

"We don't know. Some young woman. Blond hair. Blue eyes. Rather slender waist, but lots above the waist and quite a bit below. About—oh, somewhere along twenty-seven. Blue eyes. Tight-fitting blue sweater. . . . Does that ring any bell?"

"That much of it rings too many bells, Mr. Mason. I know lots of girls that description would fit. How did it happen? Was she the woman Mr. Conway was to meet, the one who called herself Rosalind?"

"We don't know," Mason said. "I haven't time to give you a lot of information. I have too many things to do between now and nine o'clock tomorrow morning. *You're* going to have to give *me* information. Now, about that voice. I understand there was something vaguely familiar about that voice, about the tempo of it?"

She nodded.

"All right. Let's think," Mason told her.

"I've been trying to think. I . . . I'm so worried about Mr. Conway, I'm afraid— Oh, I just had a feeling it was a trap."

"You like him a lot?" Mason asked.

She suddenly shifted her eyes. Her face colored. "He's very nice," she said. "However, he doesn't encourage personal relationships at the office. He's always very courteous and very considerate but— Well, not like Mr. Farrell."

"What about Farrell?" Mason asked.

"Farrell!" she spat suddenly with dislike in her voice.

"What about him?" Mason asked. "I take it he's different from Conway?"

"Very different!"

"Well," Mason said, "you're going to have to quit thinking about Conway, and start thinking about that voice, if you want to help him. You're going to have to try and place what it was about the voice that was familiar."

She shook her head. "I've been thinking and thinking, and somehow it just eludes me. Sometimes I feel that I almost have it and then it's gone."

"All right," Mason said, "let's start doing some methodical thinking. Rosalind, whoever she was, promised to deliver lists of those who had sent in their proxies."

She nodded.

"Therefore," Mason said, "she was either baiting a trap for Conway—and the way it looks now she was baiting a trap—or she was offering genuine information. In either event, she had to be someone who was fairly close to Farrell.

"If she was baiting a trap, then she was Farrell's tool, because the Farrell crowd would be the only ones who would wish Conway any bad luck. If, on the other hand, she was acting in good faith, then she must have had access to information that only some trusted employee of Farrell's would have."

Eva Kane nodded.

"It was a woman's voice," Mason said. "Did it sound young?"

"I think so. I think it was a young woman."

"Are many young women close to Farrell?"

She laughed and said, "Mr. Farrell is very close to many young women. Mr. Farrell is a man with restless hands and roving eyes. He doesn't want any one woman. He wants women—plural. He doesn't want to settle down and have a home, he wants to satisfy his ego. He wants to play the field."

"A little difficult to work for?" Mason asked.

"It depends on the way you look at it," she said drily. "Some of the girls seem to like it. And to like him."

"He's married?"

"Yes, he's married, but I understand they separated a month ago."

"What kind of woman is his wife?"

"Very nice. She's—" Abruptly Eva Kane sucked in her breath. Her eyes became wide. "That's it, Mr. Mason! That's it!"

"What is?"

"The voice. Rosalind! It's Evangeline Farrell!"

"Now, wait a minute," Mason said. "You're certain?"

"Yes, yes! I knew all along there was something about it that— I've talked with her on the phone, when Mr. Farrell was with us. She has that peculiar trick of holding onto one word for a beat and then speaking rapidly for five or six words, then pausing and speaking rapidly again."

"She was trying to disguise her voice on the phone?" Mason asked.

"Yes. The voice was disguised. It was— Oh, very sweet and seductive and syrupy and— But that little trick of timing. That's distinctive. That was Evangeline Farrell."

"She's not getting along with her husband?"

"So I understand. They've separated. It was— Oh, it's been a month or so ago. There was something in the paper about it. One of the gossip columnists had an article. She walked out on him and—I don't know what did happen. I don't think she's filed suit for divorce. Maybe she wants a reconciliation."

"Do you know where she lives?" Mason asked.

"They had a rather swank apartment and . . . and I think she was the one who moved out. I think she left him."

"No divorce?"

"Not that I know of."

"Grounds?"

"There should be lots of them. Around us girls at the office he didn't even bother to be subtle about it."

"Where can I get her present address?"

"I may have it in our address book. You see, she's a stockholder in the Texas Global. Because of the proxy fight, I've made lists of the names and addresses of all stockholders of record. There's one at the office, Mr. Conway has one, and I have one."

"Here?"

"Yes. I keep mine with me at all times."

"How does it happen she's a stockholder?"

"Part of Mr. Farrell's compensation while he was with us was in stock, and those shares of stock were turned over to his wife."

"When he got them, or as a result of some property settlement?"

"When he got them. He likes to keep all his property in

the name of some other person. But I think she wrote about them after the separation. I'm certain we had a letter giving a new address."

"See if you can find that address," Mason said.

She said, "Pardon me," went to a desk, pulled out a large address book, thumbed through the pages, then said, "I have it. It's the Holly Arms."

"I know the place," Mason told her. "She's living there?"

"Yes. Do you want to talk with her on the phone?"

He thought a moment, then said, "No, I'd better surprise her with this. Thanks a lot, Miss Kane."

"Is there anything I can do—to help?"

"You've done it."

"If Mr. Conway phones, should I tell him that I think I know the voice?"

"Tell him nothing," Mason said. "Not over the telephone. You can't tell who's listening. Thanks a lot. I'm on my way."

CHAPTER FIVE

MASON PICKED UP the house telephone in the lobby of the apartment hotel.

"Mrs. Farrell, please."

The girl at the switchboard was dubious. "I beg your pardon. It's after ten o'clock. Was she—?"

"She's expecting the call," Mason said.

"Very well."

A moment later a woman's voice said, "Hello."

Mason said, "I'm an attorney, Mrs. Farrell. I'd like to see you on a matter of some importance."

"Are you representing my husband?"

"Definitely not."

"When did you wish to see me?"

"Right away."

"Right away? Why that's impossible . . . ! What is your name, please?"

"Mason."

"You're not—not *Perry* Mason?"

"That's right."

"Where are you, Mr. Mason?"

"I'm downstairs."

"Are you—? Is anyone with you?"

"No."

"May I ask why you want to see me?"

"I'd prefer not to discuss it over the telephone," Mason said. "I can assure you it's a matter of some urgency and it may be to your advantage."

"Very well. Will you come on up, Mr. Mason? I'm in lounging pajamas. I was reading and—"

"I'd like to come right away, if I may."

"All right. Come on up. You have the number?"

"I'll be right up," Mason said.

Mason took the elevator, walked down a corridor, pressed his finger against the mother-of-pearl button beside the door of Mrs. Farrell's apartment. Almost instantly the door was opened by a striking, redheaded woman who wore Chinese silk lounging pajamas, embroidered with silken dragons. There was the aroma of Oriental incense in the apartment.

"Mr. Mason?" she asked.

Mason nodded.

She gave him her hand. "How do you do? Won't you come in?"

Mason found himself in the living room of an apartment which had at least two rooms.

Lights were low, and there was an air of scented mystery about the place.

The brightest spot in the room was where a silk-shaded reading lamp cast subdued light on a deep reclining chair and footstool.

An opened book lay face down on the table near the arm of the chair.

"Please be seated, Mr. Mason," Mrs. Farrell said, and then when Mason had seated himself, glided across to the easy chair, dropped into its depths with a snuggling motion and picked up a long, carved, ivory cigarette holder, which contained a half-smoked cigarette.

She took a deep drag, said, "What is it you want to talk with me about, Mr. Mason?"

"About Texas Global and the proxy battle."

"Oh, yes. And may I ask why you're interested?"

"I'm representing Jerry Conway."

"Oh!"

"Why did *you* want to talk with him?" Mason asked.

"Me? Talk with Mr. Conway?"

"That's right."

She chose her words carefully. "I don't want to talk with him. I know Mr. Conway. I like him. I have great confidence in his business management. I suppose you know, Mr. Mason, that my husband and I have separated.

"I expect to file suit for divorce on grounds which— Well, frankly, Mr. Mason, you're a lawyer and you understand those things. The grounds may depend somewhat on the type of property settlement which is worked out."

"There is considerable property?" Mason asked.

"As to that," she said, "there are two ways of thinking. Gifford Farrell is a gambler and a plunger. There *should* be quite a bit of money, but Gifford's attorney insists that there is very little."

"However, he has an earning capacity?" Mason said.

"Yes. He's accustomed to doing big things in a big way."

"Therefore," Mason pointed out, "it would be very much to your interest to see that he wins out in this proxy fight."

"Why do you say that?"

"Because then he would be in clover financially."

She took a deep drag on the cigarette, exhaled, said nothing.

"Well?" Mason asked.

"I would say that was a fairly obvious conclusion, Mr. Mason."

She extracted the end of the cigarette from the ivory holder, ground it out in the ash tray.

"May I fix you a drink, Mr. Mason?"

"Not right now," the lawyer said. "I'm sorry I had to call at such a late hour. If you can give me the one piece of information I want, I can be on my way."

"I didn't know I had any information that you wanted, Mr. Mason, but— You say you're representing Mr. Conway?"

"That's right."

"And you're here in his behalf?"

"Yes."

"What is it you want to know?"

Mason leaned forward in his chair. "How it happens that, if you're trying to negotiate a property settlement with your husband and want to get the most you can out of it, you offered to give Jerry Conway information on the number of proxies that have been received to date by the proxy committee?"

"Mr. Mason, what on earth are you talking about?"

"You know what I'm talking about," Mason said. "I want to know why, and I want to know why you disguised your voice and took the name of Rosalind."

She sat perfectly still, looking at him with startled slate-gray eyes.

"Well?" Mason asked.

"Why, Mr. Mason, what makes you think that I would do anything like that?"

Mason said impatiently, "Come, come! You used a telephone. Calls can be traced, you know."

Startled, she said, "But I didn't use *this* telephone. I—"

Abruptly she caught herself.

Mason said nothing, continued to regard her with steady, penetrating eyes.

She said, "Well, I guess that did it. I seem to have walked into your trap."

Mason remained silent.

"All right," she said suddenly. "I'll tell you. I'm a stockholder of Texas Global. I have a fair block of stock in that company. I have a feeling that that stock is about all of the financial nest egg I'm going to get, and if Gifford Farrell gets control of that company, I don't think the stock will be worth the paper it's written on within a period of two years. If Jerry Conway continues as president, that stock is going to be very valuable."

"Therefore, you're for Conway."

"I'm for Conway, but I don't dare let it be known. I don't dare do anything that could be seized upon by Gifford's attorneys and twisted and distorted into evidence that they could use against me. I— Mr. Mason, how *did* you find that I made those calls?"

"That's quite a long story," Mason said. "Something has happened that makes it quite important to get at the facts in the case. Now, you sent Conway to the Redfern Hotel. Why?"

"*I* sent him to the Redfern Hotel?" she asked.

"That's right."

She shook her head.

"Yes, you did," Mason said. "You had him running around so as to ditch persons who were supposed to have been shadowing him. Then you telephoned him at six-fifteen and told him to—"

"*What* did I tell him at six-fifteen?" she asked.

"You know," Mason told her. "You told him to go to the Redfern Hotel and ask for messages for Gerald Boswell."

She picked up the ivory cigarette holder and began twisting it in nervous fingers.

"Didn't you?" Mason asked.

"I did not, Mr. Mason. I don't know anything about the Redfern Hotel. I didn't tell Mr. Conway to go there."

"What did you tell him?" Mason asked.

She hesitated thoughtfully.

Mason said, "I think it's going to be to your advantage to confide in me, Mrs. Farrell."

"All right," she said suddenly, "you seem to know enough. I'm going to have to trust to your discretion. You *could* place me in a very embarrassing position if you let Gifford know what I had done."

"Suppose you tell me just what you did do."

"I wanted to give Mr. Conway some information I had. I had a list of the persons who had sent in proxies. I thought it was an accurate, up-to-the-minute list that would be of the greatest value to him. I wanted him to have that list."

"Why didn't you mail it to him?"

"Because I was afraid someone knew that I had this list. If it was ever traced to me, and then my husband could prove that I had given it to the person he was fighting for control of the company, he'd use it to prejudice the court against me."

"So what did you do?"

"I intended to give him a big build-up, send him out to a motel somewhere to keep a mysterious appointment, and then phone him and tell him that I'd planted the list in his car while he was waiting. I wanted it to be handled with such a background of mystery and all that he'd think I was very, very close to Gifford and terribly frightened. I wanted to do everything as much unlike myself as I possibly could. I wanted to cover my trail so thoroughly he'd never suspect me.

"I tried to arrange a meeting with him twice. Tonight he was to ditch the shadows, go to a public telephone in a drugstore that was a couple of blocks from here. I was to telephone him there at six-fifteen."

"And you did?"

"I did," she said, "and he didn't answer."

"Are you telling me the truth?"

"I'm telling you the truth."

"You didn't get him on the telephone and tell him to go to the Redfern Hotel and ask for messages in the name of Gerald Boswell?"

She shook her head, said, "I know nothing whatever about the Redfern Hotel. I've heard the name, but I don't even know where it is."

Mason said, "You'll pardon me, but I have to be sure that you're telling the truth."

"I've told you the truth," she said, "and I'm not accountable to you. I don't propose to have you sit there and cross-examine me. I don't owe that much to Mr. Conway and I don't owe that much to you."

"Perhaps," Mason said, "you owe that much to yourself."

"What do you mean by that?"

"For your information," Mason said, "a woman was murdered at the Redfern Hotel this evening. Conway was in the suite where the murdered girl was found. He was sent there by someone who telephoned the drugstore where he was to get his final directions and—"

"So *that's* it!" she exclaimed.

"What is?"

"I lost control of him. Someone must have called him

64

there just a few minutes before I did. I called him a minute or two before six-fifteen, got a busy signal on the line. I called him at almost exactly six-fifteen, and there was no answer. I kept ringing and finally a man's voice answered. I asked if Mr. Conway was there, and he said he was the druggist in charge of the store, and that no one was there. He said a man had been there a few minutes earlier, and had left."

Mason took out his cigarette case, started to offer her one of his cigarettes.

"Thanks, I have my own," she said.

Mason started to get up and light her cigarette, but she waved him back, said, "I'm a big girl now," picked up a card of paper matches, lit her cigarette, dropped the matches back on the table.

Mason snapped his lighter into flame, lit his cigarette.

"Well?" he asked.

She said, "It's *his* phone that's tapped. It's not mine. I put in the calls from pay stations. You can see what happened. I was anxious to see that he wasn't followed. I didn't want anyone to know I had had any contact with him. Someone listened in on the conversation. What about that secretary of his? What do you know about her?"

"Very little," Mason said.

"Well, you'd better find out," she said, "because someone beat me to the punch on that telephone call and sent him to the Redfern Hotel. I was going to tell him to meet me in a cocktail lounge about a block and a half from the drugstore, but I wanted to be certain he wasn't followed."

"Do you now have an accurate list of the proxies, or—?"

"I now actually have such a list."

"May I ask how you got it?"

She smoked for a moment in thoughtful silence, then extricated herself from the chair with a quick, lithe motion, said, "Mr. Mason, I'm going to confide in you."

The lawyer said nothing.

She walked over to a bookcase, took down an atlas, said, "When a woman marries, she wants a man for her very own. She wants security. She wants a home. She wants companionship on a permanent basis."

Mason nodded.

"I should have known better than to have married Gifford Farrell in the first place," she said. "He's a playboy. He doesn't want a home, he doesn't want any one woman, and he can't give anyone security. He's a gambler, a plunger, a sport."

Mason remained silent.

Mrs. Farrell opened the atlas. She took out an eight-by-ten glossy photograph from between the pages and handed it to Mason.

Mason saw what at first seemed to be a naked woman, but after a moment saw she was wearing the very briefest of light-colored Bikini bathing suits.

Mason looked at the voluptuous figure, then suddenly started as his eyes came to focus on the girl's face. He moved over closer to the light.

Mrs. Farrell gave a short laugh. "I'm afraid you men are all the same," she said. "She's wearing a light-colored Bikini suit, Mr. Mason. She's not nude. She's *dressed!*"

"I see she is," Mason said drily.

"You have to look twice to see it."

Mason nodded. "I'm looking twice."

The photograph showed a blond young woman, with well-rounded curves, apparently the same young woman whom Mason had seen earlier in the evening lying dead on the bed in the Redfern Hotel.

"I take it," Mason said, "that you have some connection with the woman shown in the photograph."

Mrs. Farrell laughed. "I'm afraid the connection is with my husband."

Mason raised his eyebrows in silent interrogation.

Mrs. Farrell handed Mason a piece of paper which was evidently a clipping from a popular magazine. The clipping illustrated a curvacious woman clad in a Bikini bathing suit and across the top of the ad was printed in large, black letters: "SHE'LL LOVE IT." In smaller type appeared: *"And she'll love you for it.* Get these private Bikini bathing suits. A wonderful, intimate, personal present, for just the right girl."

The ad went on to extol the virtues of the specially made Bikini bathing suit.

"Yes," Mason said drily, "I've seen these ads."

"Evidently my husband answered this," she said, "purchased a suit by mail, and persuaded this young woman to put the suit on."

Mason studied the picture thoughtfully. "This is a posed picture?"

"It is."

Again Mason studied the picture.

Mrs. Farrell said, "For your information, Mr. Mason, either the suit was donned for the occasion or— Well, I'll be charitable and say that the suit was donned for the occasion. . . . Do you find her so very attractive that you're completely engrossed?"

"I'm sorry," Mason said. "I was trying to make out the background."

"Well, it's dark and out of focus. I'm afraid you can't get much from it, Mr. Mason. However, if you'll notice the pattern of the rug beneath those high-heeled shoes, which are designed to bring out the shapeliness of her legs, you'll notice a certain very definite pattern. For your information, Mr. Mason, that rug is in my husband's bedroom. Apparently, the picture was taken while I was in New York a couple of months ago."

"I see," Mason said.

"My husband," she went on bitterly, "is something of an amateur photographer. He took this picture and two others. Evidently he wanted something to remember the girl by."

"And how did you get them?" Mason asked.

"I happened to notice that my husband's camera, which is usually kept in his den, was in a dresser drawer in the bedroom. There was a roll of films in the camera and three films had been exposed. I'm afraid I have a nasty, suspicious nature, Mr. Mason. I slipped that roll of films out of the camera and replaced it with another. I turned the film to number four so that, in case my husband investigated, he wouldn't know there was anything wrong, and in case he had the films developed and found three perfect blanks, he would think something had gone wrong with the shutter, when he was taking these pictures."

"I see," Mason commented drily. "I take it that there were then two other exposed pictures on this roll?"

"Yes," she said significantly. "It was a well-exposed roll, and the model was *well* exposed."

Mason strove to keep his voice from showing undue interest. "I wonder if you've been able to locate the model?" he asked.

Mason raised his eyebrows.

"She is Rose M. Calvert, and in case you're interested, the 'M' stands for Mistletoe, believe it or not. Her father, I understand, insisted on the name. It turned out to be quite appropriate.

"Rose Calvert was an employee in the brokerage firm which handles accounts for my husband, and, I believe, for some of the officials of the Texas Global Company. My husband has a roving eye, and Rose Calvert—well, you can see from the photograph what she has."

"She's still working with the brokerage company?" Mason asked.

"Not Rose. Rose, I understand, is living on the fat of the land. She has an apartment at the Lane Vista Apartments, number 319, but I'm afraid that's just one of the perches where this young bird lights from time to time. Apparently, she drops in for mail, and to change her clothes. I've had the place under surveillance for a few days."

"There are then two other pictures?" Mason prompted.

"Two others."

Mason waited expectantly.

Mrs. Farrell shook her head. "I'm afraid not, Mr. Mason. They're indicative of a progressing friendship. Evidently this young woman doesn't have the slightest compunction about exhibiting her charms to men or to cameras."

"I'm shockproof," Mason said.

"I'm not."

Mason studied the face of the girl in the picture.

Mrs. Farrell said, somewhat bitterly, "You men are all alike. For your information, Mr. Mason, those fine curves will be blanketed in fat in another ten years."

"I'm afraid you're right," Mason said, handing back the photograph.

"My husband likes them like this," Mrs. Farrell said tapping the photograph.

Mason almost automatically glanced at the lounging pajamas.

Mrs. Farrell laughed and said, "It's all right, Mr. Mason. I don't make any secret of it. Now, how about a drink?"

"Well," Mason said, "I could be induced if you twisted my arm."

"Hold it out," she said.

Mason held out his arm.

Mrs. Farrell took hold of the wrist, held the lawyer's arm tight against her body, gave it a gentle twist.

"Ouch!" Mason said. "I'll take it! I'll take it!"

She laughed huskily and said, "All right, sit down. I'll

have to go to the kitchen. What do you like, Scotch or bourbon?"

"Scotch," Mason said.

"Soda?"

"Please."

"Make yourself comfortable," she told him, "but don't wear that photograph out while I'm gone. I am going to have use for it."

When she had left the room, Mason hurriedly moved over to the atlas in which the photograph had been concealed. He riffled through the pages but was unable to find any other photographs.

Mrs. Farrell entered the room, carrying a tray with two tall glasses.

Mason held his drink to the light. "That looks pretty stout."

She laughed. "You look pretty stout yourself, Mr. Mason. I may as well confess that you're one of my heroes. I've followed your cases with the greatest interest. I like your way of fighting."

"Thanks!" Mason said.

She raised her glass.

"Here's to crime!" Mason said.

"Here's to us!" She touched the brim of her glass to his, let her eyes rest steadily on his as she raised the glass to her lips.

Mason waited until she had seated herself, then said, "I am interested in how you were able to secure the information that you offered Mr. Conway. The list of proxies."

"Oh, that!"

"Well?" Mason asked.

She said, "Quite naturally, Mr. Mason, after I located this Rose Calvert, I became interested in her comings and goings. A couple of days ago, Rose Calvert was closeted in her apartment. It was one of the rare intervals when she was home for a fairly long period of time, and she was pounding away on a typewriter.

"I have a firm of detectives that seem to be very competent indeed. The man who was on duty managed to inspect the wastebasket at the end of the corridor from time to time, hoping that Rose Calvert would perhaps have made some false starts and he could find enough torn scraps to find out what she was writing. As it turned out, he did far better than that. Rose Calvert was evidently writing a very, very confidential document for my husband. She was instructed to make as many copies as possible and to use fresh carbon sheets with each copy.

"You know how a carbon sheet retains the impression of what has been typed, particularly if you can get the new carbon used in the first copy and there is nothing else on the sheet.

"The detective produced the sheets, and I found that I had a perfect series of carbon papers showing the typing that Mrs. Calvert was doing for my husband."

"*Mrs.* Calvert?"

"That's right. She's married and separated. Her husband lives out in the country somewhere."

"Know where?" Mason asked casually.

She shook her head. "I've heard of the place. It's out toward Riverside somewhere. . . . Would you like to see the carbons, Mr. Mason?"

"Very much," Mason said.

She put down the drink and eased gracefully out of the chair. She walked over to a desk, opened a drawer and took out several sheets of carbon paper.

"As nearly as I can tell, these are the carbon papers used in making the first copy," she said. "She was making an original and seven copies. So, of course, there were a lot of duplicate sheets of carbon paper. I carefully segregated the different sheets."

"Have you copied them?"

"I haven't had time. I've had them photostated. I intended to give Mr. Conway one of these complete sets of carbon paper. Since you're here and are his attorney, I'll give it to you."

"Thanks," Mason told her. "Thanks very much indeed."

She glanced at him archly. "Don't mention it. Perhaps you can do something for me someday."

"Who knows?" Mason said.

"You'll have to protect me, Mr. Mason. I don't want anyone, least of all Mr. Conway, to know where those carbon copies came from."

"You can trust my discretion," Mason said. "However, I'm going to have to ask a favor. I want to use your phone."

"It's in the bedroom. Help yourself."

Mason put down his glass, went to the bedroom, picked up the phone.

"Number, please?" the operator asked.

"Give me an outside line, please," Mason said.

"You'll have to give me the number. I'll get it for you."

Mason lowered his voice, gave the number of the Glade-dell Motel. When the number answered, he said, "Can you ring Unit 21?"

"Surely, wait a moment, please."

Mason waited for several seconds, then the voice said, "I'm sorry, that phone doesn't answer."

"Thanks," Mason said, and hung up.

He returned to the other room.

Mrs. Farrell was stretched out on a chaise longue, showing up to advantage through the embroidered lounging pajamas.

"Get your party?"

"No. He didn't answer."

"There's no hurry. You can try again—later."

Mason sat down, picked up his drink, took a hasty swallow, said, "This is really loaded."

He looked at his watch.

Her look was mocking.

"Now you're terribly impatient. You want to hurry through your drink. Now that you have the information you want, the documents you want, you are giving every indication of being in a hurry to be on your way. Am I that unattractive?"

Mason said, "It isn't that. It's simply that I have a lot of work to do tonight."

She raised her eyebrows. "Night work?"

"Night work."

"I was hoping that while you were here you would relax and that we could get acquainted."

Mason said, "Perhaps your husband is having your apartment watched. He might suggest that you were entertaining men in your apartment."

Again she laughed. "Always the lawyer! Now, please, Mr. Mason, don't tell anyone about the identity of Rosalind. I'm leaving it to you to protect me."

"And," Mason said, "I suppose I'm not to say anything about these pictures?"

"Not for a while," she said.

"What are you going to do with them?"

She said, "When I'm through, I'm going to see that Mrs. Calvert has plenty of publicity. If she's an exhibitionist, I'll let them publish her picture where it will do the most good."

"You seem rather vindictive," Mason said. "Do you feel that she stole your husband?"

"Heavens, no!" she said. "But I'm vindictive just the same. I feel toward her the way one woman feels towards another who—I don't know—she cheapens all of us. Before I get done with her, she'll wish she'd never seen Gifford Farrell.

"All right," she went on, laughing, "don't look at me like that. I'm a cat! And I have claws, Mr. Mason. I can be very, very dangerous when I'm crossed. I either like people or I don't. I'm never lukewarm."

Mason said, getting to his feet, "I'm sorry, but I have to leave."

Abruptly she arose, gave him her hand. "I won't try to detain you any longer. I can see you really don't want to stay. Good night."

Mason stepped out into the corridor, carrying the sheets of fresh carbon paper in a roll.

"Good night—and thanks," he said.

"Come again sometime," she invited.

CHAPTER SIX

MASON STOPPED at a telephone booth and called Paul Drake.

"Anything on the gun, Paul?"

"Hell, no! We're just getting started."

"Any identification of the corpse?"

"None so far. The police are grubbing around the hotel and can't seem to get anywhere."

Mason said, "I'm on the track of something, Paul. I'm going to have to take a chance."

"You take too many chances," Drake told him.

"Not too many," Mason said. "I take them too often."

"Well, that's the same thing, only worse."

"According to the law of averages, it's worse," Mason told him. "Now look, Paul, I'm going out to the Lane Vista

Apartments. I want to see a Rose Calvert who is in Apartment 319. For your information, she's probably going to be named as corespondent in a divorce suit by Mrs. Gifford Farrell."

"What's the lead?" Drake asked.

"Probably more of a hunch than anything else right now," Mason told him. "The point is that there *may* be a private detective sticking around trying to get a line on her.

"Can you have one of your men get out to the Lane Vista Apartments, scout the territory and see if he can find someone who looks like a detective?"

"Sure. What does he do if he finds this guy?"

"I'll be out there," Mason said, "inside of thirty minutes. I can make it from here in about fifteen minutes, and your man should be able to make it in fifteen minutes. I'll give him fifteen minutes to case the place."

"I can't guarantee anything," Drake said. "My operatives are pretty clever at spotting men who are waiting around like that, but you just can't tell what the setup is, and—"

"I know," Mason said. "I don't want the impossible. I just want to know whether the place is being watched."

"And if it is?" Drake asked.

"I want to find out about it."

"All right," Drake said, "I'll have a man there in fifteen minutes. I have a man sitting right here in the office who's good. I'll put him on the job."

"Does he know me?" Mason asked.

"He knows you by sight. He'll pick you up all right."

"All right. I'll be there within thirty minutes. I'll park my car a block or two away and walk past the entrance to the apartment without looking in. Have your man pick me up and brief me on the situation. Can do?"

"Can do and will do," Drake said.

"How long you going to be there, Paul?"

"Probably all night. At least until something definite breaks."

"Okay, I'll be calling you."

"You'd better keep your nose clean," Drake warned. "If any good private detective is out there, *he'll* recognize *you* the minute he sees you."

"That's why I want to know if he's there," Mason said and hung up.

Mason looked at his watch, noted the time, drove until he found a hole-in-the-wall restaurant that was open, sat at the lunch counter and had two leisurely cups of coffee. He paid for the coffee, entered the phone booth, called the Gladedell Motel and this time got Gerald Conway on the line.

"Where have you been?" Mason asked.

"Nowhere. Why?"

"I called and you didn't answer."

"Oh. I just ran out to a drugstore for shaving stuff and a toothbrush. What did you want?"

"I wanted to tell you I have what I think is a complete proxy list. It doesn't look too good. I'll see you tomorrow. Just sit tight."

Mason hung up and drove to a point within two blocks of the Lane Vista Apartments, where he parked his car at the curb, got out and walked along the sidewalk, walking directly past the entrance to the apartment house without hesitating.

Halfway to the next corner, a figure detached itself from the shadows and fell into step by Mason's side.

"Paul Drake's man," the figure said without turning his head.

"Let's take a look," Mason told him.

"All right. Around the corner."

"Anyone sitting on the place?"

"Uh-huh."

"Okay," Mason said, and the two walked around the corner until they came to the mouth of an alley.

The man paused, took a folder from his pocket containing his credentials and a small, fountain-pen flashlight.

Mason studied the credentials, said, "Okay, tell me about the stake-out."

"I know the guy who's waiting," the detective said. "He's from the firm of Simons & Wells. They make a specialty of serving papers."

"Did he notice you?" Mason asked.

"Hell's bells!" the man said. "I walked right into it with my chin out."

"What do you mean?"

"I know the guy who's sitting on the job. I started to case the joint. This guy was on stake-out. He knew me, and I knew him."

"You talked with him?"

"Sure. He said hello, and wanted to know what I was out on, and I asked him if he was waiting to serve papers and he said no, he was just making a preliminary survey. I asked him if I could have one guess as to the initials of the party, and we sparred around for a while. Then he admitted he was there to tail Rose Calvert. Seems like her middle name is Mistletoe." The operative chuckled. "Some name!"

"Okay," Mason said, "what about Rose Calvert? Is she in her apartment?"

"Apparently not. Hasn't been in all afternoon. She was reported to have been in yesterday. A little before ten today she called a cab, loaded a bunch of baggage and went away. She hasn't come back."

"Dolled up?" Mason asked.

"Not too much."

"Taking a powder?"

"She could have been taking a powder, all right. Quite

a bit of baggage. There's a letter in the mailbox outside the apartment, according to what this guy tells me."

"This operative has been ringing Rose Calvert's bell?" Mason asked.

"No. He found out she was out. He's waiting for her to show. However, he goes off duty at 1:30 A.M. He didn't start working until five-thirty this evening. There's no relief coming on."

"You take a look at the letter in the mailbox?"

"No. My friend told me about it."

"What did you tell your friend?".

"Told him I was interested in another case."

"Did you give him any names?"

"No, but I don't think I fooled him any."

"What about this letter?"

"It's in an envelope addressed to Rose M. Calvert and it's got a return address in the upper side from Norton B. Calvert. The address is 6831 Washington Heights, Elsinore."

"You didn't take a peek at the letter?" Mason asked.

"Hell, no! I'm not monkeying with Uncle Sam. I didn't even touch the envelope. I got my data from my friend."

"Stamp canceled and postmarked?"

"That's right. Postmarked Elsinore yesterday."

"How is the letter? Typewritten or ink?"

"Written in pencil."

"From Norton B. Calvert, eh?"

"That's right."

"Who is this Norton B. Calvert? Husband? Son? What?"

"I don't know. She's pretty young to have a son living away from home. Around twenty-seven, as I get the impression."

"Know how she was dressed?" Mason asked.

"Yes, she was wearing a tight-fitting, light-blue sweater, straight matching blue skirt, and high-heeled shoes."

Mason digested the information in thoughtful silence.

"That mean anything to you?" the operative asked.

"I think it does," Mason said, looking at his watch. "I'm going to play a hunch. What's that address in Elsinore?"

"6831 Washington Heights, Elsinore."

Mason said, "Let's see. It's about an hour to Corona and then about thirty minutes to Elsinore. That right?"

"I believe so. That won't miss it very far."

"Ring up Paul's office," Mason said. "Tell Drake to stick around until he hears from me. Have him tell Della Street to go home. Do you think this detective connected you with me?"

"Sure he did. Naturally he's dying to find out what *my* angle is. When you came along, he would have been all eyes and ears. I let you go as far as I dared before I cut in on you, but I'm satisfied he was where he could watch us. He goes off duty at one-thirty, in case you want to call without being seen. She may be in by then."

"Okay," Mason said. "Go back and watch the place so this detective can't say you quit as soon as I showed up. Try to give him a line before he leaves. Tell him you're going to be on duty all night as far as you know. When he quits at one-thirty, wait ten or fifteen minutes to make certain he's gone, and then high-tail it back to Drake's office."

"Suppose she shows?"

"She won't."

"You're sure?"

"Pretty sure. If she shows, it won't make any difference. I just want to keep from giving this private detective any blueprints of my plans."

Mason swung away from the man, walked around the block, went to where he had parked his car, got in, filled the tank with gas at the nearest service station, and took off down the freeway.

From time to time he consulted his watch, and despite the last cup of coffee, found himself getting sleepy. He stopped at Corona for another cup of coffee, then drove on.

When he got to Elsinore, he found the town completely closed up. The police station and fire station had lights. Aside from that there was no light anywhere.

Mason drove around trying to get the lay of the town. He saw a car turn into a driveway. A family who had evidently been to one of the neighboring cities at a late show got out of the car.

Mason drove up.

"Can anybody tell me where Washington Heights is?" he asked.

The man who was evidently the head of the family detached himself from the group, came over toward Mason's car.

"Sure," he said. "You drive straight along this road until you come to the first boulevard stop, then turn right, and climb the hill, the second street on the left is Washington Heights."

"Thanks," Mason told him, leaning slightly forward with his head to one side so his hat brim would be between his features and the other man's eyes. "Thanks a lot!"

Mason pushed his foot gently on the throttle, eased away from the curb.

Mason located the 6800 block on Washington Heights, but missed 6831 the first time he went down the block. It was only after he turned and came back that he found a little bungalow type of house sitting back from the street.

Mason stopped his car, left the parking lights on, and his feet crunched up the gravel walk leading to the house.

A neighbor's dog began barking with steady insistence. Mason heard annoyed tones from the adjoining house telling the dog to shut up.

The lawyer climbed up on the steps of the small porch

and groped for a bell button. Unable to find it, he knocked on the door.

There was no answer from within.

Mason knocked the second time.

Bare feet thudded to the floor in the interior of the house. The dog in the neighboring house started a crescendo of barking and then abruptly became silent.

At length a porch light clicked. The door opened a crack, held from opening farther by a brass chain which stretched taut across the narrow opening.

A man's voice from the inside said, "Who is it?"

"I'm an attorney from the city," Mason said. "I want to talk with you."

"What about?"

"About your wife."

"My wife?"

"That's right. Rose Calvert. She's your wife, isn't she?"

"You better ask *her* whose wife she is," the man said.

Mason said, "I'm sorry. I don't want to discuss the matter out here where the entire neighborhood can hear. I drove down here to see you because I feel it's important."

"What's important?"

"What I want to see you about."

"Now, you look here," the man said. "I'm not going to consent to a single thing. I'm hoping Rose will come to her senses. If she does, all right. If she doesn't, I'm not going to make things any easier for her or for that fellow who has her hypnotized, and that's final!"

He started to close the door.

"Just a moment," Mason said. "I don't want you to consent to anything. I just want to get some information."

"Why?"

"Because it's important."

"Who's it important to?"

"It may be important to you."

The man on the other side of the door hesitated, then finally said, "Well, all right. You can come in. But this is a hell of an hour to get a man out of bed to start asking questions."

"I wouldn't do it if it wasn't urgent," Mason said.

"What's urgent about it?"

"I'm not sure yet," Mason said, "and I don't want to alarm you until I am sure. I'm an attorney, but I'm not representing your wife in any way. I'm not representing anyone connected with the aspect of the case in which you're interested. I just want to get some information, and then perhaps I can give you some."

"Well, come on in."

The chain was removed and the door swung open.

The man who stood, tousle-haired and barefooted, in the entrance hallway was wearing striped pajamas. He was nearly six feet tall, slender, about thirty-two, with dark, smoldering eyes and long, black hair which had tumbled about his head.

"Come on in," he said, yawning.

"Thanks. I'm Perry Mason," the lawyer told him, shaking hands. "I'm an attorney and I'm working on a case in which it has become necessary to get some information about your wife."

"We're all split up," Calvert said shortly. "Maybe you came to the wrong place."

Mason said, "I want to talk with you."

"There's not much I can tell you about her, except that she wants a divorce."

"There are no children?"

The man shook his head.

"How long have you been married?"

"Two and a half years. Can you tell me what this is all about? I'm sorry. I may have been a little bit short with you. I wake up kinda jumpy sometimes."

Mason said, "I have something to tell you, but I want to be pretty certain I'm right before I tell you. This may take a little time. Fifteen or twenty minutes. Do you want to get some clothes on?"

"I'll get a blanket to wrap around me," the man said.

He vanished into the bedroom, came back with a blanket and wrapped it around him.

"Sit down there in that chair by the table," he told Mason.

Mason seated himself, said, "This is a nice little bungalow you have here."

The man made a little gesture of dismissal. "I rent it furnished. After we broke up, I thought for a while Rose would come back to me, but now I've about given up."

"Were you living together down here?"

"No, I moved down here about three months ago—that was right after we split up."

"What's your occupation?"

"Running a service station."

"Would you think me terribly presumptuous if I asked you to tell me about what happened in your marriage, how it happened you broke up, and—?"

"I guess it's all right," Calvert said. "We got off to a good start. We had been going together a couple of months. She was in a brokerage office. I was a salesman. We sort of clicked and we got married.

"She didn't want children right at first. We decided we'd wait on that and that we'd both keep on working.

"Then an uncle of mine died and left me quite a nest egg. Not too much. It figured about sixty thousand, by the time taxes were taken out of it. So then I felt we could start having a family."

"How much of that nest egg do you have left?" Mason asked.

Calvert's lips tightened. "I've got all of it left."

"Good boy!" Mason told him.

"And if I'd listened to her, I wouldn't have had *any* of it left," Calvert went on. "That was one of the things that started the trouble. She wanted to live it up, to travel, to get clothes, to do all the things that take money.

"I wanted to save this money to invest in something. I wanted a business of our own. I didn't want her to keep on working. I wanted children."

"Did she want children?"

"She couldn't be bothered."

"All right, what happened?"

"Well, we got along all right, but I could see the novelty of marriage was wearing off and— Rose is a woman that men notice. She has a figure and she's proud of it. She likes people to notice it."

"And they do?" Mason asked.

"They do."

"Precisely what caused the final split-up?"

"A man by the name of Gifford Farrell."

"With Texas Global?"

"That's right. He's fighting a proxy battle. There are ads in the Los Angeles newspapers. He's trying to get enough proxies to take over."

"How long has he known your wife?"

"I don't know. I don't think it was entirely his fault, but he certainly was on the make and she fell for him."

"How long had it been going on?" Mason asked.

"I tell you I don't know. I guess quite a while. I wanted to get ahead by plugging along and keeping my eye on the main chance.

"This Farrell is just like Rose. He's a gambler, a guy who shoots the works, rides around in high-powered automobiles, spends three and four hundred dollars on a suit of clothes, wouldn't think of looking at a pair of shoes that didn't cost over twenty dollars. He's a showman, likes to go out to night clubs and all of that."

"And now your wife wants a divorce?"

"That's right."

Mason took his cigarette case from his pocket. "Mind if I smoke?"

"Not at all. I'll join you. I smoke a good deal myself. Here."

The man passed over an ash tray which was pretty well filled with cigarette stubs, said, "Wait a minute! I'll empty that."

He went out into the kitchen, dumped the ashes into a wood stove, came back with the ash tray, inspected the cigarettes in Mason's cigarette case, said, "Thanks, I have my own brand."

He took a package of cigarettes from his pajama pocket, extracted one, and leaned forward to accept the light which Mason held out as he snapped his lighter into flame.

The lawyer lit his own cigarette, said, "Do you have any pictures of your wife?"

"Pictures? Sure."

"May I see them?"

"Why?"

"I want to be absolutely certain that you and I are talking about the same woman," Mason said.

Calvert looked at him for a moment, took a deep drag on the cigarette, exhaled twin streams of smoke from his nostrils, got up, walked into the other room and came back with two framed pictures and an album.

"These are pictures she had taken," he said.

Mason studied the framed, retouched photographs. "You have some snapshots?"

The man opened the album, said, "This goes back to when we first met. She gave me a camera for my birthday. Here are some of the more recent pictures."

Mason thumbed through the album. Within a half-dozen pictures he was virtually certain of his identification.

He closed the album and said, "I'm sorry to have to bring you the news, Calvert. I can't be *absolutely* certain, but I'm *practically* certain that your wife was involved in a tragedy which took place a few hours ago."

Calvert jerked bolt upright. "An automobile accident?"

"A murder."

"A murder!"

"Someone killed her."

For several long seconds Calvert sat absolutely motionless. Then his mouth twitched downward at the corners. He hastily took another drag on his cigarette, said, "Are you sure, Mr. Mason?"

"I'm not absolutely sure," Mason said, "but I think the body I saw was that of your wife."

"Can you tell me about it?"

"She was in the Redfern Hotel, lying on a bed. She was wearing a blue sweater, sort of a robin's-egg blue, and a skirt to match."

Calvert said, "That sweater was a Christmas present from me last Christmas. She likes tight-fitting sweaters. She's proud of her figure. It's a good one."

Mason nodded.

"Have they got the person who . . . who did it?"

"No, I don't think so."

Calvert said, "She was pretty well tied up with this Farrell. She was afraid of Mrs. Farrell."

"Why?"

"I don't know. I think Mrs. Farrell had threatened her at one time. I know she was afraid of her."

"You had separated for good?" Mason asked.

"I never really gave up. I thought she'd come to her senses and come back. That's why I came down here. At present I'm running this filling station. I've got a chance to buy a store here. I think there's a good living in it, but I'm a man who goes at things like that pretty cautiously. I don't act on impulse. I wanted to look this place over at first hand. The service station I have is right next door to the store. I think maybe I'll buy it. . . . How can I find out for sure about my wife?"

"Someone will probably be in touch with you within a short time, if the body is that of your wife," Mason said. "It's hard to make an identification from photographs."

Calvert pinched out the cigarette. "How did you happen to come here?" he asked. "How did you find me?"

Mason said, "There's a letter in the mailbox at her house. It had your address on the upper left-hand corner. I had to see some photographs. I thought perhaps you'd have them."

"You saw . . . saw the body?"

Mason nodded.

Calvert said, "I hadn't heard from her for six weeks, I guess. Then she wrote to me and told me she wanted to go to Reno and get a divorce."

"Did she say that she and Farrell were planning on getting married?"

"No, she just said she wanted a divorce. She said that she could establish residence in Reno and get a divorce without any trouble if I'd co-operate."

"What did she mean by 'co-operate'?"

"She wanted me to file an appearance of some sort. It seems if I get an attorney and appear in court to contest the action, they can get around a lot of red tape in serving a summons and save a lot of delay. She said she was willing to pay for the attorney."

"And what did you tell her?" Mason asked.

"I told her that I'd co-operate if she was sure that was what she wanted," Calvert said, "and then I've been thinking things over and—well, I just about decided to change my mind. When you came down here and got me up out of a sound sleep, I was mad! I made up my mind I wasn't going to fall all over myself fixing it so she could get tied up with this man Farrell. He's a fourflusher, a woman chaser—and he's just no good!"

"Do you have the letter which your wife wrote?" Mason asked.

"I have it," Calvert said. "Just a minute."

He kicked off the blanket, walked into the bedroom again, came back with an envelope which he handed to Mason.

The lawyer shook the letter out of the envelope, read:

Dear Norton,

There's no reason why either of us should go on this way. We're both young, and we may as well have our freedom. We've made a mistake which has cost us a lot of heartaches, but there's no reason for it to ruin our lives. I'm going to Reno and get a divorce. They tell me that, if you will get a lawyer and make an appearance in Reno, that will save me a lot of time and a lot of money in having the case brought to trial.

So why not be a sport and give me a break? You don't want a wife who isn't living with you, and I don't want to be tied up by marriage. That's not fair to me and it isn't doing you any good.

I'm sorry I hurt you so much. I've said this to lots of people and I'll keep on saying it: You are one of the most thoughtful, considerate husbands a girl could ask for. You're sweet and patient and understanding. I'm sorry that I couldn't have been a better wife to you, but after all each person has to live his own life. Now be a sport and let me make a clean break, so we can both begin all over.

Yours,
Rose

Calvert began twisting his fingers nervously. "I just can't seem to picture her as being dead, Mr. Mason. She's so full of life and vitality. You're sure?"

"No," Mason told him, "I'm not sure. But I *think* the woman I saw was your wife. She was blond with blue eyes, and she was wearing this blue sweater which just about matched her eyes. The eyes were only partially open, and— well, you know how it is with a dead person. Sometimes it's hard to make a positive identification from photographs, but I think I'm right."

"What was she doing at the Redfern Hotel?"

"I don't know."

"How does Gifford Farrell figure in this?"

"I don't know that. I don't even know that he figures in it."

Calvert said with considerable feeling, "Well, you can bet your bottom dollar he figures in it somewhere. I guess I could have got along without Rose all right, if I'd felt she was being happy with somebody, but this . . . this thing —it just sort of knocks me for a loop."

Mason nodded sympathetically.

Abruptly Calvert got up. "I'm sorry, Mr. Mason. You've got the information you want and I . . . well, I'm just not able to keep on talking. I feel all choked up. I guess I'm going to take it pretty hard. I tried to pretend that I could get along without her, but I always had a feeling she was coming back, and— Just pull the door closed when you leave."

Calvert threw the blanket into a crumpled ball on the floor, walked back hurriedly to the bedroom, kicked the door shut.

The house grew silent.

Mason switched out the lights, and felt his way to the door. Behind him he could hear harsh, convulsive sobs coming from the other side of the bedroom door.

The lawyer eased out of the house, tiptoed up the gravel walk. The dog in the adjoining house once more started a frenzied barking and was again calmed to silence by the man's authoritative voice.

Mason got in his car and drove back toward the city.

From Corona, Mason called Paul Drake.

"This is Perry, Paul. Any news?"

"Nothing important."

"Body been identified?"

"Not yet. At least not as far as anyone knows."

"Anything else new?"

"Sgt. Holcomb rang up and wanted to know where you could be reached."

"What did you tell him?"

"I told him I didn't know where you were, but I knew that you intended to be at the district attorney's office at nine o'clock in the morning."

"What about Della?"

"I told her you said to go home, but she didn't go. She's sticking it out. She's got a percolator full of hot coffee. . . . What the heck are you doing down at Corona?"

"Running down a lead," Mason said. "Now look, Paul, here's something I want you to do."

"What?"

"Cover the Redfern Hotel. Find out if there were any check-outs from the seventh floor between six and eight last night. If there were, I want those rooms rented by some of your operatives."

"You can't ask for a specific room by number," Drake said. "It would make them suspicious. . . ."

"Don't be that crude," Mason told him. "Have operatives go to the hotel. They're just in from a plane trip. They don't want to get too high, but they want to be high enough to be away from the street noises, something on the seventh floor. Then start getting particular until they get the rooms we want."

"Check-outs tonight? Is that right?"

"Well, it's yesterday night now," Mason said, "but I want any check-outs between—well, say between six and nine just to be safe."

"You coming in here?" Drake asked.

"I'm coming in," Mason told him. "What have you found out about the gun? Anything?"

"Not yet. We're working."

"Well, get some action," Mason told him.

"Do you know what time it is?" Drake asked.

"Sure, I know what time it is," Mason said. "And I'll tell you something for your information. By tomorrow the police will be swarming all over us. If we're going to do anything at all, we're going to have to do it before nine o'clock this morning."

"I've got ten men out," Drake said. "They should turn up something. Come on in and have a cup of coffee. I'll try to get a line on the hotel. I've got a couple of men in there already. They're buying drinks, tipping the bellboys and trying to get them to talk."

"What kind of a place?" Mason asked.

"You can get anything you want," Drake told him.

"Who runs it? The clerks?"

"The bell captains run that end of it."

"Well, we may want something," Mason told him. "I'm coming in, Paul. I'll be seeing you in an hour."

CHAPTER SEVEN

MASON'S STEPS echoed along the corridor of the silent building as he left the elevator and walked down to his office. He inserted his latchkey, snapped back the spring lock and opened the door.

Della Street, who was stretched out in the overstuffed chair, her feet propped on another chair, her legs covered with a topcoat, jumped up, blinking.

She saw Mason's face, smiled, and said, "Gosh, Chief, I was asleep. I made myself comfortable and all of a sudden I went out like a light."

"There's coffee over there in the electric percolator. I'm afraid it's pretty strong and stale by now. I made it fresh about midnight."

"Didn't Drake tell you to go home?"

"He told me you *said* to go home," Della Street smiled. "But I thought I'd wait it out, at least until you got in."

"What have you got to go with the coffee?" Mason asked.

"Doughnuts. And they're pretty good. I went down to this doughnut shop just before it closed at midnight and got a bag of fresh doughnuts. . . . I'll bet I'm a mess."

She shook out her skirt, put her hand to her hair, fluffed it out, smiled at Perry Mason.

"What's new?"

"Lots of things, Della. Give Paul Drake a ring and ask him if he wants to come down and have coffee, doughnuts and chitchat."

Della Street promptly put through the call, said, "He's coming right down."

Mason opened the closet which contained the washstand, washed his hands and face in hot water, rubbed briskly with a towel.

Della Street produced three big coffee mugs and opened the faucet on the electric percolator. The office filled with the aroma of hot coffee.

Drake's code knock sounded on the door.

Della Street opened it.

"Hi, Paul," Mason said, hanging up the towel with which he had been drying his face. "What's new?"

"Not too much at this end," Drake said. "What's new with you?"

"They're going to have the body identified in about thirty minutes," Mason said.

"How do you know?"

Mason grinned. "I fixed a time bomb so it will go off just about on schedule."

"How come?"

"The body," Mason said, "is that of Rose Calvert. Rose's middle name, believe it or not, was Mistletoe. Her dad thought she might turn out to be romantic. His hunch was right—poor kid.

"For your information, Rose's husband, Norton B. Calvert, lives in Elsinore, is running a service station, and was waiting from day to day in hopes that his wife would come back.

"Probably at about this time he's at the Elsinore police station, telling them that he has reason to believe his wife has been murdered, and asking the Elsinore police to find out about it. They'll call the Los Angeles police, and since there is only one unidentified body, at least so far, the police will ask for a description, and very shortly will have an identification."

"But won't they find out that *you* were down there?" Della Street asked apprehensively.

"They'll find out I was down there," Mason said, "and they'll be mad. They'll feel that I held out on them in respect to an identification of the body."

"Well?" Drake asked drily. "Wouldn't that be a natural conclusion under the circumstances?"

"Sure, it will," Mason said. "So the police will decide to give my client the works. They'll check on Rose Calvert, and find out that during the last few weeks of her life she had been very, very much involved with Gifford Farrell. They will, therefore, jump at the conclusion that Farrell is my client. They'll descend on him, and they'll probably be rather inconsiderate and ungentle.

"Find out anything about that gun, Paul?"

"Not yet. That information is supposed to be available only during office hours, at least to the general public. However, I took it on myself to issue a gratuity of fifty dollars and I'm expecting—"

"Well, grab this coffee while it's hot," Della Street said, "and you can do your expecting right here."

Drake said dubiously, "I've been swigging down coffee all night."

Mason picked up one of the big mugs, put in sugar and cream, stood with his feet apart, leaning slightly forward. He reached for a doughnut, then raised the coffee mug to his lips.

"How is it?" Della Street asked apprehensively.

"Couldn't be better," Mason said.

"I'm afraid it's stale and bitter."

"It's wonderful!"

Drake tasted his coffee, said, "Well, you have to admit one thing, it's strong."

"I need it that way," Mason said. "At nine o'clock I'm going to have to face an irate district attorney, and by that time the police are going to feel I've pulled at least one fast one on them."

The telephone rang, and Della Street said, "That's probably your office calling you now, Paul."

Drake put down his coffee mug and picked up the telephone.

"Hello," he said. "Yes, yes, this is Drake talking. . . . How's that again . . . ? Hold the phone a second." Drake looked up at Della Street and said, "Make a note, will you, Della? Pitcairn Hardware & Sporting Goods. Okay, I've got it. What's the date? September second, three years ago. Okay." Drake hung up the telephone, said, "Well, we've got the gun located. I don't know whether this is going to do you any good or not, Perry."

"What do you mean?" Mason asked.

"The gun was sold to the Texas Global for the protection of a cashier. The signature was that of the cashier, but the charge was made to the company itself on an order made by Conway.

"You can see what that does. It brings that weapon right home to Jerry Conway."

Mason thought for a moment, then a slow grin suffused his features. "That," he said, "brings the gun right home to Gifford Farrell. Gifford Farrell was with the company at that time, and was taking a very active part in the office management."

"What do you think happened?" Della Street asked.

Mason stood holding his doughnut in one hand, his coffee mug in the other.

"What I *think* happened is that Gifford Farrell had a fight with his sweetheart and probably caught her cheating. He lost his head, pulled a gun and fired. Or it may have been that Rose Calvert found Gifford was cheating and committed suicide. In any event, Farrell must have had Conway's telephone tapped. He knew that Conway was going to a public telephone booth to get directions at six-fifteen. Farrell took a chance. He had a girl call in at six-twelve, and Conway was there a few minutes early waiting for the other call. So Conway took the wrong message and was gone by the time the real message came in. Conway was just like a guided missile that's being directed by radio. When he got to a certain point, someone with another more powerful radio stepped in, took control and sent the missile off on an entirely new path."

"Well," Drake said, "it's a two-edged sword. Remember that both Farrell and Conway could have had access to the fatal weapon."

"It's all right," Mason said, "unless—"

"Unless what?" Della Street asked.

"Unless," Mason said, "Conway got smart and decided to— No, he wouldn't do anything like that. . . . However, I didn't take the number of the gun when he first showed it to us. It wasn't until after he was down at the motel I wrote down the number. . . . Anyway, it's all right. We'll go down to see the D.A. in the morning, and there'll be nothing to it. He can't make a case against Conway now, and he's going to be afraid to try. What did you find out about check-outs, Paul?"

"There was only one check-out at the hotel between six and nine from the seventh floor."

"What time was that check-out, Paul?"

"About six-fifty."

"Who was it?"

"A young woman named Ruth Culver."

"The room number?" Mason asked.

"728."

"Where is that with reference to 729?"

"Directly across the hall."

"Have you got that room sewed up?" Mason asked.

"I have an operative in it right now. He'll stay until we give him the word."

"What have you found out about the Culver girl?"

"I've got men working on her. She's in her twenties with auburn hair, a fairly good-looking babe. . . . Here's the strange thing, Perry. She checked in about ten in the morning, then left just before seven that night."

"Did she make any explanation as to how she happened to check out at that time?"

"She said she'd had a long-distance call. Her father who lives in San Diego is very ill."

"Baggage?" Mason asked.

"Quite a bit of it."

Mason said, "Check the San Diego planes, Paul. Find out if one of them had a passenger named Ruth Culver, and—"

"Now look," Drake interrupted, "you don't have to do *all* my thinking for me, Perry. That's routine. However, the clerk thinks this girl said she was going to drive down."

Mason finished his doughnut, held out his mug for a refill.

Della Street turned the spigot and let coffee trickle into the mug.

"What about your operative up in Room 728? Can I trust him?" Mason asked.

"You can trust him unless the police start putting pressure on him," Drake said. "None of these operatives are going to stand up to the police, Perry. They need the good will of the police to keep working."

"What's the name of this operative in Room 728?"

"Fred Inskip."

"Does he know me?"

"I don't think so."

"Give him a ring," Mason said. "Tell him that I'm going to come up sometime before noon. Tell him to leave the door unlocked. I want to take a look in there. . . . How about the police? Have they cleared out?"

"They've cleared out," Drake said. "They sealed up Room 729."

Drake watched Mason as he picked up another doughnut, said, "How I envy you your stomach, Perry! I've ruined mine sitting up nights living on soggy hamburgers and lukewarm coffee. Somehow when coffee is lukewarm, you drink four or five cups of it. If you can get it piping hot, you don't drink so much."

"Why don't you get one of these big electric percolators?" Mason asked.

"Let me have Della Street to run it and keep house, and I will."

Mason grinned. "Don't talk like that, Paul. You could get yourself shot. Ring up Inskip and tell him to expect me around—oh, say ten or eleven."

Drake put his coffee mug down on a piece of blotting paper, dialed a number, said, "I want to talk with Mr. Inskip in 728, please. Yes, I know it's a late hour, but he's not in bed. He's waiting for this call. Just give the phone the gentlest tinkle if you don't believe me."

A moment later, Drake said, "Fred, this is Paul. I won't mention any names, because I have an idea someone is monitoring our conversation, but a friend of mine is coming up to see you around ten o'clock. Leave the door unlocked. . . . Okay."

Drake hung up the telephone, said to Mason, "Remember, Sgt. Holcomb is looking for you. Are you going to try to get in touch with him?"

"He'll be in bed by this time," Mason said. "I wouldn't want to disturb his beauty sleep."

"Now look," Drake warned, "remember this about Inskip. He isn't in a position to hold out on the police if they start asking specific questions. You've been around the hotel, and someone may recognize you."

"It's all right," Mason said. "I don't care if they know I've been there after I've left. The only thing I *don't* want is to have some smart guy like that room clerk, Bob King, ring up the police and say that I'm there and am visiting someone in Room 728. That might be what you would call premature."

"To say the least," Drake said drily. "Della, please put those doughnuts out of sight. They tempt me, and I'd have my stomach tied up in knots if I tried to keep up with your ravenous employer."

Mason said, "I guess this just about winds things up, Della. How about getting in your car and driving home?"

"What are you going to do?"

"I'm going to run out to my apartment, shave, take a shower, and maybe get a couple of hours' sleep before I have to go pick up Conway."

"All right," she said, "I'll go home."

"Don't bother with straightening things up here now. You can do it in the morning. Come on, I'll go down with you and see that you get in the car. Pull that percolator plug out of the socket, and leave everything until morning."

"The office looks a wreck."

"What do we care?"

Mason held Della Street's coat for her. They switched out lights, and Mason, Della Street, and Paul Drake walked down the corridor.

"You going to call it a day, Paul?" Mason asked.

"Gosh, no!" Drake said. "I'm sitting in the middle of everything up there. I have to be where I can handle the telephones."

"Can you get any sleep?"

"I don't think so. I'll keep right on."

"You'll have some stuff to do tomorrow—that is, I mean later on in the day."

Drake said, "It's all right, Perry. I work right on through lots of times. That's what's wrong with my stomach."

"Well," Mason told him, "I think we've got this case pretty much under control. We'll go up there and make an appearance at the D.A.'s office as a matter of form, but— Say, wait a minute, Paul. They should know who the corpse is by this time. Let's check."

"All right. Step in my office," Drake said.

They followed Drake into his office. Drake asked the switchboard operator, "Anything new on that murder case at the Redfern Hotel?"

"Nothing except the calls I relayed down there."

"They haven't identified the body?" Drake asked.

"Not as far as *we* know."

Drake looked at Mason.

Mason said, "That fellow was pretty well caved in. I sure gave him pretty much of a jolt, but I felt he'd have been in touch with the police long before this time."

"It could have happened without our knowing it," Drake said. "I've got one of the newspaper reporters on the job. He telephones anything in to his paper first and then he'll give it to me second. If he got an exclusive scoop, he probably wouldn't want to trust me with the information until after the paper was on the street. But on anything routine that the other reporters would pick up, he'd call me just as soon as he'd finished talking with the rewrite man at the desk."

"Well, they probably know by this time, but aren't announcing it to the press," Mason said. "They've probably sent for the husband to come and make an identification. They'll sure be looking up the boy friend. Well, I'll put Della in her car and go on to my apartment. I'll be seeing you, Paul."

Mason took Della Street's arm. They left the office, rode down silently in the elevator.

Mason escorted her over to the parking lot and put her in her automobile. "I don't like to have you driving around the streets alone at this hour, Della."

"Phooey! I'll go home like a streak. No one's going to bother me. I am out at all hours of the day and night on this job."

"I know you are," Mason said. "And I wish you weren't. You take too many chances driving around a city at this hour of the morning."

She patted his hand. "Thanks for the thought, Chief, but I'm fine. Don't worry. I put the windows up, lock the doors, use the mechanical signal and don't stop until I get to the apartment. I'll be seeing you."

"I'll follow you in my car, Della, see you safely home and—"

"You'll do nothing of the sort! You need every minute of sleep you can get. Good night!"

Della Street stepped on the starter, switched on the lights and drove out of the parking lot.

Mason got in his own car, gunned the motor to life and raced after her. He caught up with her five blocks down the street.

The brake lights on Della's car blazed red as she swung in to stop at the curb. Mason drew alongside, rolled down the window on his car.

"Chief, you go home! I'm just as safe as can be. You shouldn't be—"

Mason rolled up his window, sat waiting with the motor running. At length Della gave up and pulled out from the curb.

Mason followed her to her apartment house. She parked the car, came over to where Mason was waiting.

Again the lawyer rolled down his window.

"Chief," she said in a low voice.

"Yes?" He leaned out to hear her better.

She said, "Custom decrees that when a man has taken a girl home, he is entitled to a token of thanks."

Before he caught the full import of her words, she had kissed him full on the lips, then turned and ran up the steps of her apartment house.

"Thank you," she called to him as she opened the door.

"Thank *you!*" Mason said.

CHAPTER EIGHT

IT WAS FIVE MINUTES after eight when Mason swung his car into the Gladedell Motel and drove to Unit 21.

Jerry Conway was waiting for him.

"All ready?" Conway asked. "Shall I follow you in my car?"

"Wait a minute," Mason told him. "We're going to have to do some talking. I'll drive my car down the road for a couple of blocks then pull into the curb. I'll park my car there and drive in with you."

"How about having me go in your car?"

"No, the police will want to search *your* car."

"I've searched it," Conway said, "and I've found something that bothers me."

"You've *found* something?"

"Yes."

"What?"

"It was under the front seat where a man ordinarily wouldn't look once in a couple of years. It was a neatly typed list of the stockholders who had sent in their proxies."

FREE

ot 2-Not 3... But 6
Mason THRILLERS

Postage
Will be Paid
by
Addressee

The Detective Book Club

Roslyn, L. I.
New York

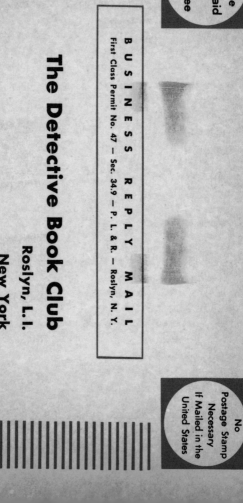

No
Postage Stamp
Necessary
If Mailed in the
United States

"Let me look at it," Mason said.

Conway handed him four typewritten sheets of paper neatly stapled together. He said, "It was there under the front seat where it might seem I had tried to conceal it where it wouldn't be found. It was in a manila envelope."

"How did it get there?"

"I don't know. It could have been put there any time."

"While you were parked near the hotel?"

"While I was parked near the hotel, while I was parked in front of the drugstore where I was telephoning, while I was parked anyplace."

"You keep your car locked?"

"No, I take the ignition key with me, of course, but the doors and windows are unlocked."

"What about the list? Have you checked it?"

"As nearly as I can. There's one peculiar thing about it."

"What?"

"It's almost *too* good."

"What do you mean, almost too good?"

"Almost too reassuring. The people who have sent in proxies are, for the most part, the very small shareholders, and some of them I know were discontented, anyway. They'd have sent in proxies even if there hadn't been any advertising campaign."

"On a percentage basis what does it figure?"

"As nearly as I can figure without having access to the books of the corporation, there's only about 17 per cent of the outstanding stock represented on this proxy list."

"Any date on it?"

"Yes, it's dated only a couple of days ago. It's supposed to be right up to date."

"How much have you handled it?"

"Handled it? Quite a bit. Why?"

"Then you've probably obliterated any chance of tracing it," Mason said.

"What do you mean? You can't get fingerprints from paper, can you?"

"Sometimes you can," Mason said. "Using iodine fumes, you can quite frequently bring out latent fingerprints."

"I didn't handle the envelope much. I've gone over the list pretty thoroughly."

"I'm afraid it's part of the trap," Mason said. "Let's get started and I'll tell you about *my* information. You've had breakfast?"

"Sure, I had breakfast early this morning. I didn't sleep much last night."

"Who did?" Mason asked.

"You were worried?" Conway asked in alarm.

"I was busy," Mason told him. "Come on, let's get started."

"What about your list of stockholder proxies, and why do you think my list is a trap?" Conway asked.

Mason produced the sheets of carbon paper from his brief case. "Take a look at these and you can see for yourself."

"Where did you get these?" Conway asked.

"Straight from the horse's mouth."

Conway held the sheets of carbon paper to the light one at a time, studied them carefully.

When he had finished he said, "If these are the straight goods, Mason, I'm licked."

"That bad?"

"That bad."

"These *could* be phony," Mason said, "but I don't think so."

"What will I do with that other list, the one I found in my car?"

"You'll have to give it to the D.A. Tell him you found it when you searched your car. *You* don't know where it came from so you'll have to tell him the whole story. They'll be searching your car this morning."

"Do I tell him anything about these sheets of carbon paper you have?"

"Not unless you want a one-way ticket to San Quentin."

"You're damned mysterious, Mason. I'm your client."

"That's why I'm being mysterious. I'm going to get you out of this, but I'll do it my way."

"That's a promise," Conway said. "Let me tell them I'm checking out. Then you drive your car down the street and I'll pick you up."

"Okay," Mason said. "We've got lots of time."

Mason drove a block before he found a parking space. He slid his car into the curb, put the ignition keys in his pocket, took his brief case and moved over to Conway's car.

Conway was preoccupied, thinking about the proxy battle. "I'm afraid those ads have done more damage than I realized," Conway said.

"Of course," Mason pointed out, "the ads have been running for a while, and most of the people who would be swayed by that type of reasoning would already have sent in their proxies. Don't throw in the sponge. . . . You have that gun with you?"

"Yes. . . . How *did* you get that list, Mason?"

"It's a long story," Mason told him, "and we haven't time to discuss it now. We're going to have to go to the district attorney's office, and you'll have to tell your story. You're going to be questioned, and the newspaper reporters are going to have a field day."

"That will suit Farrell just fine!" Conway said bitterly.

"Don't be too certain," Mason said. "I think Farrell is having troubles of his own."

"How come?"

"I planted a couple of time bombs on him," Mason said. "The police haven't made any public announcement as yet, but I think they've identified the corpse."

"Who is she?"

"A Rose Calvert who worked in a brokerage office, and—"

"Rose!" Conway exclaimed.

"Do you know her?"

"Of course I know her. She works in the brokerage office that handles my accounts. That is, she did work there. I think she left two or three months ago. I haven't seen her for a while."

"You used to talk with her?"

"Yes."

"Kid her along?"

"Yes."

"Ever date her?"

"You aren't kidding?"

"No."

"She's married, Mason. It's *Mrs.* Calvert."

"And you never dated her?"

"No."

"Never tried to date her?"

"No."

"But you did kid her along?"

"She liked to kid. She was jolly and liked attention from the customers."

"The masculine customers," Mason said.

"That's right. She had a good figure and she knew it."

"All right," Mason said. "Now, here's where you let your hair down and tell me the truth. Did you try to do any gun juggling?"

"What do you mean?" Conway asked.

"I know it was a temptation," Mason said. "You felt that you had been framed. You felt that Gifford Farrell was back of it. You didn't want to sit still and take it. You probably felt that if you could get rid of that fatal gun and substitute another gun in its place, there was no way on earth they could ever prove that it *was* the fatal gun that you had taken away from that girl."

Conway said, "You've probably been reading my mind."

"All right," Mason told him, "what did you do about it?"

"Nothing. You're my lawyer. I followed instructions."

"You didn't try to switch guns?"

"No."

"You were tempted?"

"I thought of it."

Mason said, "In a case of this kind, you really can't tell what to do. If you switch guns, you've got the other people in an embarrassing position. They can't swear that the guns have been juggled without disclosing their own guilty knowledge.

"The whole crux of their frame-up depends upon getting *you* to tell a story that sounds improbable on the face of it, something that sounds like a desperate attempt to account for having the fatal gun in your possession, as well as a list of stockholders which somehow must have been taken from Rose Calvert. You add to that the fact that you asked for mail under an assumed name, went up to a room in which the body was subsequently found, entered that room with a key, and it builds up to a pretty darned good case of first-degree murder."

"It gives me the creeps to hear you summarizing it," Conway said.

"Well, don't worry too much about it," Mason told him, "because there's one weak point in the case."

"What's that?"

"They had to force you to take the fatal gun," Mason said. "The weak link is that the fatal gun can be traced."

"You've traced it?"

"Yes."

"Who bought it?"

"You did."

"What?" Conway shouted. "What are you talking about?"

"You bought it," Mason said. "At least you authorized its purchase."

"What are you talking about? I never saw this gun before in my life."

"That may be," Mason said, "but apparently some three years ago the cashier convinced you that he needed a gun for protection, and you authorized the purchase of a weapon at the Pitcairn—"

"Heavens, yes! I remember it now," Conway said, "but I never even saw the gun. The voucher came through, and I put my okay on it. The cashier was the one who went down and bought it."

"What happened to that cashier?" Mason asked.

"He died eight or ten months later."

"While Farrell was with the firm?"

"I believe so."

"And what happened to the gun?"

"That I don't know."

"You didn't check it?"

"Good Lord, Mason, the Texas Global has options on potential oil land scattered halfway across Texas. I'm trying to figure where the oil deposits are, how much we can afford to pay, how deep we should go with our wells. . . . I had no time to go take an inventory of the property in the desk of a cashier who dies suddenly."

"Exactly," Mason said. "That's the weak point in the scheme. Farrell had just as good access to the gun as you did, and when it comes to proving motivation or having connection with the corpse, Farrell is in a *very* delicate position. He had been playing around with this young woman, had taken photographs of her in the altogether, and his wife was planning to name her as corespondent in a divorce suit."

"Oh-oh," Conway said.

"So," Mason told him, "if *your* nose is clean, and if you didn't try to get smart by juggling weapons between the time you left Drake's office and the time I took the number off that gun, I think we can get you out of it. I know we can put you in such a position that the district attorney won't dare to proceed against you without more evidence."

Conway drove for a while in silence, then said, "Mason, don't underestimate Gifford Farrell. He is not a sound thinker, but he has a chain-lightning mind. He'll completely dazzle you. He'll reach some conclusion after seemingly brilliant thinking, and then, for some cockeyed reason or other, the conclusion will turn out to be unsound."

"I know the type," Mason said.

"Well, don't underestimate him," Conway pleaded. "He's clever, he's ingenious, and he's utterly ruthless."

Mason nodded.

"Now, what do I do at the district attorney's office?" Conway asked.

"You tell them the truth," Mason said. "Unless I stop you, keep on talking."

"Tell them the *entire* truth?"

"The entire truth."

"That might call for a little thought here and there."

"It calls for nothing," Mason said. "You have no guilty knowledge of the crime. You know what happened, and your job is to convince the officers. The minute you start getting cagey and trying to withhold something, or emphasizing one fact and minimizing another, trying to spread gilt paint over the truth, they'll know exactly what you're doing. They've had so much experience with liars, they can just about tell when a man starts lying."

"All right," Conway said, "I'll tell them the truth. But I'm worried about that gun."

"I was at first," Mason told him, "but I'm not any longer. When it comes to a showdown, we can probably prove that Farrell took that gun out of the cashier's desk, or at least had more opportunity than you did."

Conway thought things over for several minutes, then said, "Mason, I'm afraid that you may be trying to over-simplify this thing."

Mason lit a cigarette. "Just quit worrying, tell the truth, and leave the rest to me," he said.

CHAPTER NINE

PROMPTLY AT NINE O'CLOCK Mason held the door of the district attorney's office open for Jerry Conway.

"Perry Mason and Mr. Conway," he told the secretary at the outer desk. "I told the police I would be here at nine o'clock with my client to answer questions. We're here."

The girl at the desk said, "Just a moment!"

She picked up the telephone, put through a call, then said, "You may go in, Mr. Mason. Right through those swinging doors and all the way down the corridor, the office on the far left."

Mason and Conway walked down the long corridor, opened the last door on the left.

Hamilton Burger, the big, barrel-chested district attorney, sat behind the desk facing the door. He was flanked by Lt. Tragg, one of the most skilled investigators in the Homicide Department, a uniformed police officer, and

Alexander Redfield, who did ballistics work for the authorities.

The spools of a tape recorder on the table were revolving slowly.

Hamilton Burger said, "Good morning, gentlemen. I have decided that this interview should be recorded. I trust there is no objection?"

"None whatever," Mason told him.

"Thank you," the district attorney said sarcastically. "I may also state for your information that there is a microphone in this office, and the conversation is also being monitored by a police shorthand reporter."

"Quite all right," Mason said. "This is my client, Gerald Conway, gentlemen."

"Sit down," Hamilton Burger invited. "What is your occupation, Mr. Conway?"

"I'm president of the California & Texas Global Development & Exploration Company."

"As I understand it, you had occasion to consult Mr. Perry Mason sometime last night?"

"Yes, sir."

"Do you remember the time?"

"It was, I believe, shortly before seven o'clock."

"And how did you get in touch with Mr. Mason?"

"I looked up a night number in the telephone exchange, called it, was directed to the Drake Detective Agency, and so managed to get in touch with Mr. Mason."

"And what did you want Mr. Mason to do?"

"I wanted him to advise me in connection with a disturbing incident which had happened in the Redfern Hotel."

Hamilton Burger glanced suspiciously at Mason. "You're going to let him tell his full story?"

"I'm going to let him tell his full story," Mason said.

"All right, go ahead," Hamilton Burger said. "Go right ahead."

Conway told about the mysterious telephone calls, about the offers to give him the list of stockholders who had given proxies to Gifford Farrell's proxy committee. He told about his hesitancy, his final decision to have a meeting with the mysterious Rosalind.

He told about calling in his secretary to take down the conversation, about going out and following instructions to the letter, about the telephone call which had been received while he was waiting at the booth in the drugstore.

Conway then went on to tell about his trip to the Redfern Hotel.

Mason said, "Just a minute. I want to interrupt for a couple of questions."

"Later," Hamilton Burger said. "I want to get his story now."

"I'm sorry," Mason said, "but you have to know a couple of things in order to understand the full import of that story. About the time element, Mr. Conway, you had been told that the telephone would ring at six-fifteen?"

"That's right."

"When *did* the telephone ring?"

"It was a few minutes earlier than that."

"What difference does that make?" Hamilton Burger asked.

"It makes a lot of difference, as I will be prepared to show later on," Mason said. "Now, one other thing, Mr. Conway, when that call came in, that is, the one you received at the drugstore, it was a woman's voice, was it not?"

"Yes."

"Was it the same voice that you had heard earlier? In other words, was it the voice of the woman who had described herself as Rosalind?"

"That's another point. I didn't think it was at the time, and the more I think of it, the more certain I am that it wasn't."

Mason said, "I don't think my client understands the full import of this, gentlemen. But the point is that the woman who described herself over the telephone as Rosalind was going to call Mr. Conway at six-fifteen and tell him to go to a certain place to get the information he wanted. When she called the pay station at six-fifteen, there was no answer. The reason was that Mr. Conway had already received his erroneous instructions and was then on his way to the Redfern Hotel."

"Why would someone give him erroneous instructions?" Lt. Tragg asked.

"You be the judges of that," Mason said. "Now, go on, Conway, and tell them what happened."

Conway described his trip to the hotel, the envelope that he had received containing the key to Room 729. He told of going up to the room, knocking at the door, receiving no answer, then being tempted to retrace his steps, turn in the key, and call the whole thing off.

However, he pointed out, the prospect of getting the information which would be of the greatest value to him was too much of a temptation. He had used the key, had gone in. With dramatic simplicity he described in detail his adventure with the young woman who was clad only in the scantiest of apparel.

Then Conway described the panic which had gripped him when he realized the weapon he had taken from the young woman had been fired once, and recently. He decided he should consult Perry Mason.

"And what did Perry Mason advise you to do?" the district attorney asked.

Mason interposed with an urbane smile, "At this point, gentlemen, my client's story ends, except for the fact that he found a paper containing a list of stockholders who had sent in their proxies in his car. This list which I now hand you contains Conway's initials on each page, and also my initials are on each page.

"My client's car is parked downstairs, and I reported that fact to the police before we came up and suggested they would want to search the car.

"My client has nothing to say about anything that happened *after* he consulted me. I am perfectly willing to answer questions from that point on. However, you must realize that the advice of an attorney to a client is not anything which can be produced in evidence, and questions about it should not be asked."

Hamilton Burger's face slowly purpled. "As a citizen, you're bound by laws the same as anyone else. Whenever you try to conceal a weapon with which a murder has been committed—"

"A murder?" Mason asked.

"A murder!" Hamilton Burger shouted. "A murder was committed with that weapon!"

"But I didn't know it! I didn't know there had been a murder. Conway didn't know there had been a murder. He only knew that he had taken possession of a weapon under circumstances which made the whole thing look suspiciously like a frame-up. He called on me to investigate. I investigated."

"But as soon as you investigated," Burger said, "you went to that room and encountered a corpse."

"That's right."

"And then you knew that the gun was the murder weapon!"

"Indeed I did not!" Mason said. "*I* didn't know it was the murder weapon. I don't know it *now*."

"The hell you don't!" Burger shouted. "Anyone with

the intelligence of a two-year-old kid would have known it, and you're not that big a fool. Where's the gun?"

Conway took the gun from his pocket and passed it across to Hamilton Burger. "It's loaded," he said.

Burger looked at the gun, handed it to Alexander Redfield.

The ballistics expert looked at the gun, swung open the cylinder, looked at the exploded shell, took a sharp, pointed engravers' tool from his pocket and etched on the shells the relative position which they occupied in the cylinder of the gun. Then he snapped the cylinder shut, and dropped the gun in his pocket.

"Now then," Hamilton Burger said, "I want to know what happened last night. I want to know where this man was all night."

"What does that have to do with it?" Mason said.

"It has a lot to do with it," Burger said. "He resorted to flight."

"To flight!" Mason said.

"You're damned right he did!" Burger said. "Don't think the police are entirely dumb, Mason. We found out about Conway a short time ago, after we had identified the corpse. We found out that Conway had gone up in the elevator of your office building last night, that he had gone to Paul Drake's office, that an hour or so later your estimable secretary, Della Street, came up in that elevator, that shortly afterward Conway went down and just a few moments later Della Street went down. I think the inference is fairly obvious. You had telephoned Della Street to get your client out of circulation."

"But why should I want him out of circulation?" Mason asked.

"So he couldn't be questioned."

"Then why should I bring him here this morning?"

"Because now you've had time to concoct a story!"

"I'm sorry, Mr. District Attorney," Perry Mason said, "but your suspicions are not justified by facts. There was no flight. Mr. Conway simply felt that it would be inconvenient for me to consult with him during the night at his apartment. I was doing some investigative work, trying to find out the extent of what I felt was a frame-up. Therefore, I had Mr. Conway wait at a place where he would be more available and where I could call on him at night without disturbing anyone or attracting undue attention.

"Mr. Conway, for your information, gentlemen, was at the Gladedell Motel. He occupied Unit 21, and I'm quite certain you will find that he registered under his own name. It is certainly not flight for a person to go to a motel and register under his own name, driving his own car, and registering the correct license number of that car."

"All right!" Burger shouted. "Then why did you withhold this evidence until nine o'clock this morning?"

"What evidence?"

"This gun! The one that Redfield has. The murder weapon."

"But I don't know it's a murder weapon," Mason said. "I knew that you wouldn't be at your office until nine o'clock in the morning. I made arrangements with Mr. Conway to come here at the earliest possible hour this morning. We arrived just as soon as your office opened. In fact, I think an investigation would disclose that you are here unusually early this morning because you wanted to question my client."

"That's just a run-around," Hamilton Burger said. "You should have given this weapon to the police last night, and you know it."

"Why?"

"Because a murder was committed with it."

"Oh, I certainly hope not," Mason said. "Oh, I certainly

116

do hope not, Mr. District Attorney. That would complicate matters!"

"You mean you didn't have the slightest idea that this was a murder weapon?" Burger asked sarcastically.

"How would I know it was a murder weapon?" Mason countered. "No one even told me how the young woman died. They told me to get out of the room and stay out of the room. The police didn't reveal the result of their investigations to me. Was she killed with a revolver?"

"She was killed with a revolver, and this is the murder weapon, the one which you folks were concealing from the police all night."

Alexander Redfield cleared his throat. "May I say something, Mr. Burger?"

"Not now!" Burger said. "I demand that Mr. Mason give us an explanation."

Mason said, "There isn't any explanation because I am not prepared to concede the premise on which you are acting. *I* don't know that it's the murder weapon. I did feel that an attempt was made to frame my client with a gun which had been discharged somehow. I wanted to try and find out something about that gun and where it came from."

"And you did?" Hamilton Burger asked.

"I did," Mason said. "For your information, that is a revolver which was purchased some three years ago by the Texas Global Company for the protection of its cashier.

"I can assure you, gentlemen, that I have been quite busy trying to get information in this case so that I could be of some assistance to you this morning."

"You went to Elsinore last night!" Hamilton Burger charged.

"That's right. I did indeed!"

"Why?"

"Because I felt there was a possibility Mr. Norton B. Calvert, who lives in Elsinore, could shed some light on the identity of the corpse."

"All right," Hamilton Burger said sarcastically. "Now tell us just what intuitive reasoning made you think he could shed light on the identity of the corpse?"

Mason said, "Mr. Burger, I will answer that question if you tell me that you are asking that question in your official capacity, and that as a citizen and as an officer of the court it is my duty to answer."

"What are you trying to do?" Hamilton Burger asked.

"I'm trying to protect myself," Mason said. "Do you tell me that such is the case?"

"I tell you such is the case. Answer the question."

"Very well," Mason said. "I felt there was a great possibility that, if there had been a frame-up—and mind you, I say *if,* gentlemen, I am not stating that there was a frame-up. I am simply stating that if there had been a frame-up —there is always the possibility that frame-up might have something to do with the Texas Global proxy fight.

"With that in view I did a lot of investigative work last night and I learned that Gifford Farrell had been taking a great interest in a Rose M. Calvert. I learned that the description of this young woman matched perfectly the description of the young woman whose body I had seen in the hotel bedroom. Therefore, I decided to go to see Rose Calvert's husband and see if I could find some photographs of his wife. I felt that perhaps such a trip would disclose important information."

"And that is the reason you went to see the husband?" Lt. Tragg asked, suddenly curious.

"That is why I went to see him."

"How did you get his address?" Tragg asked.

"I was advised," Mason said, "that there was a letter in the letter box at the Lane Vista Apartments where Rose Calvert has her apartment, addressed to her and bearing the return address of Norton B. Calvert of 6831 Washington Heights, Elsinore."

"How did you know that letter was there?" Hamilton Burger asked.

"I was advised it was there."

"By whom?"

"By a detective."

"And he looked at that letter?" Burger asked.

"No, sir. I don't think he did. I think he in turn was advised by another detective, who was shadowing the apartment at the request of still another party."

"Mrs. Farrell?" Lt. Tragg asked.

"I didn't say that, Lieutenant. I didn't mention any names. I am simply trying to tell you how it happened I went to Elsinore. I have been ordered to answer that question and I am trying not to withhold information. I don't want you to think I am making any accusations. I am only exposing my mental processes."

"Well, you seem to have had a remarkably brilliant flash of inspiration or intuition, or mental telepathy or psychic ability, or whatever you want to call it," Hamilton Burger said sarcastically. "The body was that of Rose Calvert, but *we* didn't know it until about six o'clock this morning. You evidently had the information some hours before we did, and did nothing about it."

"I didn't have the information," Mason said. "I saw pictures and I noticed that there was quite a resemblance. I told Mr. Calvert that I was very much afraid his wife had been the victim of a tragedy. I felt that if he wanted to pursue the matter further, he would get in touch with the police.

"However, you can appreciate my position. I certainly couldn't start saying that Rose Calvert had been murdered, and then have it appear the whole thing was a hideous mistake, and Rose Calvert would show up alive and well.

"Making an identification of a corpse whom you have seen only once from snapshots is rather a ticklish matter as you, Lieutenant, undoubtedly realize."

"You're being very conservative all at once," Hamilton Burger said.

"I wanted to be sure," Mason said.

"Moreover," Burger went on, "you aren't telling us the truth about how you secured the husband's address."

"What do you mean?"

"There wasn't any such letter in the mailbox."

"I was advised that there was."

"Well, there wasn't."

"I'm sorry," Mason said, "but that's how I got the address. . . . I was told the letter was there."

Hamilton Burger turned to Redfield. "Redfield," he said impatiently, "get to your laboratory and test that gun. Fire test bullets from it. Identify it as the fatal weapon. At least let's get that done. That's what you're here for."

Redfield made no move to leave his chair. "May I say something, Mr. District Attorney?" he asked.

Hamilton Burger, his patience worn thin, shouted, "Well, what the hell do you want to say? That's the second time you've made that crack."

"And I was told not to say anything," Redfield said.

"Well, if you have anything to say, for heaven's sake, say it and then start checking on that bullet."

Redfield said, "This gun is not the murder weapon. The fatal bullet which killed Rose Calvert was fired from a Colt revolver. A Colt has six grooves which are inclined to the left. This is a Smith & Wesson revolver and, for your information, it has five grooves which are inclined to the right.

"I knew as soon as Mr. Conway passed over this gun that it couldn't possibly have been the murder weapon."

"What?" Hamilton Burger shouted.

Lt. Tragg half-rose from his seat, then settled back.

120

Mason strove to keep a poker face. He looked sharply at Conway.

Hamilton Burger seemed to be trying to get his ideas oriented.

Suddenly he said, "So that's it! It's the same old razzle-dazzle. Mason has taken this murder weapon and switched it. He's had his client turn in this other gun, and is acting on the assumption that no one can disprove his story without producing the young woman from whom Conway says he took this gun. . . . And the minute that is done, there will be confirmation of Conway's story. . . . This is a typical Perry Mason razzle-dazzle!"

"I resent that!" Perry Mason said.

"Resent it and be damned!" Hamilton Burger shouted. "I've seen too many of your slick substitutions, your sleight of hand, your—"

"Just a minute," Mason interrupted. "Don't be foolish. I am perfectly willing to resort to some forms of unconventional action for the purpose of checking the testimony of a witness. However, I certainly would not be party to any substitution of a murder weapon and then have a client tell you a lie about it."

"Poppycock!" Hamilton Burger said.

For a moment there was a silence. Everyone seemed to be at an impasse. Abruptly Burger picked up the telephone and said, "Bring Gifford Farrell in here, please."

The door from an anteroom opened, and Sgt. Holcomb of Homicide Squad escorted a debonair individual into the district attorney's office.

"Mr. Gifford Farrell," the district attorney announced.

Farrell was in his thirties, a tall, broad-shouldered, thin-waisted, well-dressed individual. His face was bronzed with outdoor living. A hairline mustache emphasized the curve of his upper lip. He had smooth, dark eyebrows, dark, glittering eyes, so dark that it was impossible to distinguish the pupils. His hair was cut so that sideburns ran a couple of inches below his ears. He was wearing a brown plaid sport jacket, and gabardine slacks.

"You know Mr. Conway," Hamilton Burger said.

Farrell's thin lips came away from even, white teeth in a smile. "Indeed I do," he said. "How are you this morning, Jerry?"

"Good morning, Giff," Conway grunted.

"And this is Mr. Perry Mason," Hamilton Burger said. "He has just accused you of trying to frame his client, Mr. Conway."

Farrell's lips clamped shut, his glittering, dark eyes regarded Mason with cold hostility.

"I have done nothing of the sort," Mason said smoothly. "I have simply pointed out to the district attorney that I felt my client was the victim of a frame-up."

"Well, you said that it was a frame-up over this proxy battle in Texas Global," Burger said.

"I did indeed," Mason said. "And I am quite willing to state that I think the probabilities are—mind you, gentlemen, I say the *probabilities* are—that the attempted frame-up was because of that proxy battle, and if there was a frame-up, then I believe there is a possibility Mr. Farrell should be considered suspect."

"There you are," Hamilton Burger said.

Farrell kept his eyes on Mason and said, "I don't like that."

Mason surveyed the man from head to foot and said calmly, "No one asked whether you liked it or not."

Farrell took a quick step toward Mason. The lawyer made no move.

"Just a minute!" Hamilton Burger said.

Farrell stopped his advance.

Hamilton Burger said, "Farrell, what do *you* know about a gun that was purchased by the Texas Global Company for the protection of its cashier? The gun was purchased three years ago."

Farrell frowned in concentration, shifted his eyes from Mason to Burger, said, "I'm afraid I know nothing, Mr. Burger."

"Now, think carefully," Burger said. "The gun was purchased, and I understand was turned over to the cashier who—"

"Do you know who okayed the invoice?" Farrell asked.

"Mr. Conway has admitted that he probably did."

"I said I thought I might have," Conway corrected.

Once again Farrell's teeth flashed. "Well, gentlemen, there's your answer!"

Mason said, "I take it you knew the young woman who was found dead in the Redfern Hotel, Mr. Farrell?"

Farrell's eyes were impudent. "What if I did?"

"You knew her rather intimately, I believe."

"Are you making an accusation?"

"I am asking a question."

"I don't have to answer your questions. I'll answer questions asked by the police and by the district attorney."

"This Rose Calvert was doing some work for you?" Hamilton Burger asked Farrell.

"Yes, sir. She was. She was doing some very confidential work. It was work that I didn't want to entrust to a regular stenographer. I wanted someone who was outside of the business, someone whom I knew I could trust. I chose Mrs. Calvert.

"Now, I will say this, gentlemen. In some way it leaked out that she was doing this work, and an attempt was made to get her to deliver information to Mr. Conway. Conway offered her five thousand dollars in cash for copies of the work she was doing, listing the stockholders who had sent in their proxies. She refused the offer."

Conway said angrily, "That's a lie! I never talked with

her in my life—that is, about that work. I didn't know she was doing it!"

Farrell said, "I have her assurance that you did."

The district attorney looked at Conway.

"That's an absolute falsehood," Conway said. "I never rang up Mrs. Calvert in my life. I knew her only as a young woman who was in the brokerage office where I transacted my individual business and much of the business of the Texas Global. I used to chat with her, in the way one would chat with an employee under conditions of that sort. I didn't know her otherwise."

"How well did Farrell know her?" Mason asked.

"I'll conduct this inquiry, Mr. Mason," Burger said.

"In case you're interested," Mason told him, "Mrs. Calvert's husband says that Gifford Farrell knew her quite well; in fact, too well."

"And that is a falsehood!" Farrell said. "My relations with Rose Calvert were a combination of business and friendship."

"Ever buy any clothes for her?" Mason asked.

Farrell said, "I did not, and anyone who says I did is a damned liar!"

"Then," Mason said, "I have talked with a liar who says that you bought her a Bikini bathing suit. You sent a mail order to one of the magazines that advertises those things. However, there's no use questioning your word, because the mail-order records will show that."

Farrell's face showed startled surprise. His eyes which had been glaring at Perry Mason suddenly shifted. He became conscious of the circle of men who were regarding him with keen interest, their trained eyes taking in every flicker of facial expression.

Farrell took a deep breath, then once more his teeth flashed in a quick smile. "I'm afraid, Mr. Mason, that you have been making a mountain out of a molehill. It is true,

I did send away for one of those Bikini bathing suits. It was just a gag. I intended to use it as the basis for a practical joke in connection with one of my associates.

"I can assure you that the suit had nothing to do with Rose Calvert."

"Then how did it happen," Mason asked, "that she put the suit on?"

"She didn't!" Farrell snapped.

"Then how did it happen that you took her picture with the suit on, a picture which was posed in your bedroom while your wife was in New York?"

Try as he might, Farrell couldn't keep the dismay from his face.

There was a long period of silence.

"Well?" Hamilton Burger asked. "We're waiting, Farrell."

Farrell said, "I don't know what the idea of this is. I came up here to do anything I could to help find the murderer of Rose Calvert. I didn't come up here to be cross-examined by some attorney who is trying to shield the murderer and drag a lot of red herrings across the trail.

"There has been a lot of talk about frame-up, and I guess perhaps I have been unusually naive. I don't know who is trying to frame something on me, but if this question is going to hinge upon some Bikini bathing suit which I purchased as a joke, and some accusations in regard to pictures, I guess I had better get an attorney of my own."

"Do you deny that you took such a picture?" Mason asked.

Farrell faced him and said evenly, "Go to hell."

Mason grinned at Hamilton Burger. "The canary seems to have quit singing and started chirping."

Sgt. Holcomb said, "I've had a long talk with Farrell, Mr. Burger, and I'm convinced that he's all right. Perry Mason is just trying to use this business as a red herring."

Hamilton Burger said abruptly, "I see no reason for letting this interview degenerate into a brawl. Conway has appeared and has told his story. The gun which he has handed us and which he insists he took from the Redfern Hotel is quite obviously not the fatal gun."

"Not the fatal gun!" Farrell exclaimed.

Burger shook his head.

"Then he's switched guns!" Farrell said.

"You don't need to point out the obvious to this office," Hamilton Burger said with dignity. "Mr. Mason's legal ingenuity is too well known to need any comment from anyone.

"I desire to interrogate Mr. Farrell further.

"Mr. Mason and Mr. Conway are excused. Just go on out and I will send for you again if there are any further developments."

Mason took Conway's arm. "Come on, Jerry."

Mason opened the door. Conway and Mason walked out together down the long corridor and out through the folding doors into the district attorney's waiting room. The office was jammed with newspaper reporters. Flashbulbs popped in a dazzling array of blinding light flashes.

Reporters crowded around asking questions.

Conway tried to force his way through the reporters.

"Take it easy, Jerry," Mason said. And then to the reporters, "We'll make a statement to you, gentlemen. An attempt was made to frame a murder on my client, Gerald Conway. I don't know whether the murder was committed and then the murderer, in desperation, tried to involve Mr. Conway, or whether the whole thing was part of a scheme to discredit Conway in connection with this battle for proxies in the Global Company. I can only tell you gentlemen what happened, and assure you of our desire to co-operate in every way possible in cleaning up this case."

"Well, what happened?" one of the reporters asked.

Mason turned to Conway and said, "Tell them your story, Jerry."

Conway frowned and hesitated.

"It's a damned sight better to let the newspaper have *your* version," Mason said, "than to get a second-hand, garbled version from someone who was present in the district attorney's office—Gifford Farrell, for instance."

Conway again related his story, while reporters crowded around making notes and asking questions.

CHAPTER TEN

CONWAY, driving Mason back toward the Gladedell Motel so the lawyer could pick up his car, said, "That wasn't so bad! How did I do, Perry?"

"You did all right," Mason told him. "I think you made a good impression on the newspaper boys and that's going to mean a lot. Fortunately, you had a chance to tell the reporters your story first. By the time the district attorney gets done questioning Gifford Farrell and he has a chance to talk with the reporters, the story of your interview will have been written up."

"It was worth a lot watching Giff Farrell's face when you sprung that on him about the Bikini bathing suit," Conway said.

Mason nodded. "Of course, Jerry, the fact that a man has been buying a Bikini bathing suit for a girl doesn't mean that he murdered her."

"Well, he could have murdered her, all right."

"And," Mason went on, "you have to remember that we don't *know* it was murder. She might have committed suicide. The thing I can't understand is about that gun."

"What about it?"

"It wasn't the murder weapon."

"Boy oh boy! Wasn't it a grand and glorious feeling when that expert spoke up?" Conway said. "That let me right off the hook!"

"I'm not so certain," Mason told him. "It's a complication that I can't understand and I don't like it."

"Why?"

Mason said, "That woman *wanted* you to take that gun from her. She didn't intend to shoot you. She came out of the bedroom stripped down to the minimum in order to put you at a disadvantage. All she had to do was to start screaming, and you would have been at a terrific disadvantage. You realized that and wanted out of there the worst way. She drew that gun and then kept advancing toward you. Her hand was shaking. There's no question about it; she wanted you to take that gun!"

Conway said, "Thinking back on it, I'm not so sure it wasn't just plain panic on her part."

"She walked out of a room where there was a corpse," Mason pointed out. "She pulled a gun out of the desk and kept advancing on you, holding out the gun so that it was an invitation for you to grab it."

Conway, feeling expansive with relief, said, "She may have been nervous. Perhaps she got blood on her clothes in shooting her roommate and wanted to change her clothes and get rid of the blood-spattered garments. She was in the process of doing that when I walked in the room. Naturally she was in a terrific panic."

"So she pulled a gun on you?"

"That's right."

"And what did she want when she pulled the gun?"

"She was afraid I was going to— Well, perhaps she was afraid I was going to take her into custody."

"She didn't tell you to get out," Mason said. "She told you to hold up your hands. The thing just doesn't make sense."

"Well, we're out of it now," Conway said.

Mason remained silent.

Conway drove for a while in silence, then said, "Well, here's your car."

"Wait a minute," Mason said, "that's a police car parked up there in the next block. Let's see what they're doing. Drive by slowly, Jerry."

Conway drove up to the next block.

"Oh-oh," Mason said, "they're searching the motel grounds with mine detectors."

"What's the idea of that?" Conway asked.

"The idea of that," Mason told him drily, "is they think you substituted weapons and disposed of the murder gun while you were down here at the Gladedell Motel. . . . Look over there to the left. Quick!"

One of the searchers had thrown down the mine detector and was calling excitedly to the others.

A group of people from two police cars converged around him. For a moment, as Conway drove by, Mason had a brief glimpse of a man holding a revolver out at arm's length. A pencil was placed down the barrel of the gun he was holding so that any fingerprints would not be smirched.

There was only the one brief glimpse of that scene, and then Conway's car had slid on by. Conway put a foot on the brakes.

"Keep going! Keep going," Mason said.

"That man had a gun," Conway exclaimed.

"Sure he had a gun," Mason remarked, "and what's more he dug up that gun from the yard in back of the motel where you admitted staying last night. Now then, Conway, suppose *you* tell *me* the truth."

"What do you mean?"

Mason said, "You got smart. You buried the gun they gave you. Then you went to your office and got this other gun. You substituted guns so you wouldn't have the fatal weapon in your possession."

"I did no such thing!" Conway retorted angrily, slowing down.

"Keep driving!" Mason told him. "Stop now and we're sunk."

Conway said, "I am not a fool, Mason. I put myself in your charge. I asked for your advice. I took it and—"

"All right! All right!" Mason said. "Shut up. Let me think for a minute!"

"Where do you want to go?" Conway asked.

"Drive around the block," Mason said. "Take me back to my car, and—"

A siren sounded behind them.

"All right," Mason said. "Pull over to the curb, and get a story ready. They've evidently recognized us."

However, the siren was merely being used to clear the traffic. The police car coming from behind rocketed on past with steadily accelerating speed.

Mason said, "They're rushing that gun to the crime laboratory for testing."

"But how could Giff Farrell have known where I was going to be so he could plant that gun down here?" Conway asked.

Mason said, "You took elaborate precautions to see that you weren't followed *to* the Redfern Hotel. But you didn't take precautions to see that you weren't followed *from* the Redfern Hotel."

"There wasn't anybody there to follow me," Conway said. "I had ditched the shadows."

"If it was a frame-up," Mason pointed out, "they would have been waiting for you at the Redfern Hotel and have shadowed you from there to Drake's office, then out. In that way they'd have known you spent the night at the Gladedell Motel. What a slick scheme it would be to have you take a gun which you actually thought was the murder weapon, go through all the agony of trying to decide what to do, tell your story to the district attorney, and then have it appear that *you* had switched guns during the night."

Conway thought for a moment, then said bitterly, "I told you this Gifford Farrell was ingenious."

"That," Mason said, "makes a beautiful, beautiful frame-up."

Conway turned the corner. "All right. What do we do?"

"We sit tight," Mason said. "We wait for the breaks, and if they've pulled that sort of frame-up on you, I'm going to have to use every ounce of ability and mental agility I can command to get you out of it."

"Well, that's Gifford Farrell for you," Conway said. "That's a typical Farrell idea! I told you the guy was brilliant."

Mason said, "Get me to my car, Conway! I've got work to do."

"Then what do I do?"

"Go to your apartment," Mason told him. "They'll drag you in for questioning as soon as they've tested that gun at ballistics. If it's the fatal weapon, you're going to have a charge of first-degree murder placed against you."

"Hang it!" Conway said. "I should have known Farrell wouldn't stop with a simple frame-up. That guy always does things with what he likes to refer to as the artistic touch."

"There's one thing that Farrell didn't count on," Mason pointed out. "That's the roll of undeveloped film in his camera and the fact that his wife has those pictures. I can see now why that knocked him for a loop."

"And what do I do if they charge me with first-degree murder?" Conway asked.

"You put the matter in my hands," Mason said.

Conway abruptly slid his car into the curb. "I can't go any farther, Perry. I'm shaking like a leaf. I know now what's happened. I know what it means. Even if they don't convict me of murder, it will mean the end of Texas Global as far as I'm concerned. Proxies will be pouring in on Farrell like falling snowflakes."

"Get yourself together," Mason said. "Pull out and drive up as far as my car. I haven't time to walk. Now, just remember one thing. If they bring you up and confront you with the murder weapon, and if they say they're going to charge you with first-degree murder, demand that they bring the case to trial before this stockholders' meeting. Insist that it's a frame-up on account of the proxy fight and demand vindication.

"Okay, now, get yourself together and start driving!"

CHAPTER ELEVEN

IT WAS NEARLY NOON when Perry Mason parked his car near the Redfern Hotel.

He bought a paper, opened it and then walked rapidly to the door leading to the lobby.

As he pulled back the door, Mason held the paper in front of him as though engrossed in some article on the sporting page.

He walked at a leisurely, steady pace to the elevator.

"Seven," Mason said, holding the paper so that he could see only the legs of the girl elevator operator, his face completely concealed from her by the paper.

The cage started upward.

Abruptly she asked, "Where's your friend?"

"How's that?" Mason asked.

"The one who was interested in my book."

Mason lowered the newspaper, looked at the girl with interest. "Oh," he said, "it's you. What are you doing here?"

"Running the elevator."

"So I see. Do you work twenty-four-hour shifts?"

"Eight-hour shifts. We switch shifts every two weeks. This is shift day. I started work at 5:00 A.M. and go off duty at one o'clock."

"How did you recognize me?" Mason asked curiously.

"From your feet."

Mason regarded his shoes thoughtfully. The elevator came to a stop at the seventh floor.

"What about my shoes?" Mason asked.

"Not your shoes. Your feet."

"I thought you were interested in that book you were reading."

"I was, but I notice people's feet and—well, I noticed your friend. Where is he now?"

"He's in his office—or he was the last I saw of him."

"Is he married?"

"Not him."

She said, "I like him."

"I'll tell him," Mason said.

"No, no, don't do that! I didn't mean it *that* way. I meant. . . ."

Mason laughed as her voice trailed off into silence.

"All right," Mason said, "what about my feet?"

"It's the way you stand," she said. "You keep your feet flat on the floor and evenly spaced like a man getting ready to slug somebody. Most people lounge around with their weight on first one foot and then the other or lean against the rail along the edge of the elevator. You stand balanced."

"Thanks for telling me," Mason said. "I'll try to be more average after this."

"Don't do that," she said.

"Why not?"

She smiled at him. "You're too distinctive the way you are."

Mason regarded her thoughtfully. "But you fell for my friend," he said.

"Who said I fell for him?"

"Didn't you?"

She pouted a moment, then said, "Well, perhaps a little. You're different. You're inaccessible. But your friend is more . . . well, more available. Now, if you tell him any of this, I'm going to put scratch marks all over your face."

"Can I tell him you're interested?" Mason asked.

"No," she said shortly.

"When did you quit last night?" Mason asked.

"Gosh, not only did I have to switch shifts this morning, but I had to work later last night because of the trouble. They wanted to question the other girls."

"When you say the trouble, you're referring to the murder?" Mason asked.

"Hush! We're not supposed to even mention that word." The buzzer on the elevator sounded.

"Well, thank you," Mason said, "I'll tell my friend."

She looked up at him impudently. "Where are you going?"

"What do you mean?"

"Here on the seventh floor?"

The buzzer rang again.

"You'd better get the elevator back down," Mason said.

She laughed. "That's what I mean by being inaccessible. You've been talking to me, not because you were interested in *me*, but because you don't want me to know what room you're going to. You were stalling around waiting for me

134

to start down. All right, smartie, I said you were inaccessible. Go ahead."

She slid the elevator door closed, and took the cage down.

Mason walked down to Room 728 and turned the knob.

The door swung open. A man who was seated in a straight-backed chair which had been tilted against the wall, his stocking feet on the bed, a cigarette in his mouth, looked up at Mason and nodded.

Mason kicked the door shut.

"You're Drake's man?" Mason asked.

The man said, "Hello," tonelessly, cautiously.

Mason walked over to stand by the individual who got to his feet. "You know me. I don't know you," Mason said.

The operative opened his wallet and showed his identification papers. "How thoroughly have you gone over this place?" Mason asked.

"I've taken a look," Inskip said. "It's clean."

"Let's take another look," Mason told him. "Got a flashlight?"

"In my bag there."

Mason took the flashlight, bent over and carefully followed the edges of the worn carpet around the room. He gave careful inspection to the washstand in the bathroom.

"You sleep here?"

"I'm not supposed to sleep until I get an okay from Drake. He told me you were going to be in this morning. I was looking for you earlier. I didn't want to go to sleep until after you'd been here. When you leave, I'll put a 'Don't Disturb' sign on the door and get eight hours' shut-eye. However, I'll be available in case anyone wants anything."

Mason said, "On a check-out they'd make up the bed before they rented the room."

"Sure!" the man said.

"Okay," Mason told him. "Let's take a look at the bed. You take that side, I'll take this. Just take hold of the bot-

135

tom sheet and lift the whole thing right off onto the floor. I want to look at the mattress."

"Okay," Inskip said, "you're the boss."

They lifted the sheets and blankets entirely off the bed. Mason studied the mattress carefully.

"I don't know what you're looking for," Inskip said, "but I heard that the bullet didn't go clean through. Death was instantaneous and there wasn't any bleeding except a little around the entrance wound. That was all absorbed by the sweater."

"Well, there's no harm in looking," Mason said.

"You don't think anything happened here in *this* room, do you?" Inskip asked.

"I don't know," Mason told him.

The lawyer moved the flashlight along the edge of the mattress.

"Give me a hand," he said to Inskip. "Let's turn this mattress over."

They raised the mattress.

"Any stain on the mattress would have had to soak through the sheets, and bloodstained sheets would have been reported," Inskip said.

"I know," Mason said. "I— Here! What's this?"

"Well, I'll be damned," Inskip said.

They propped the mattress on its edge and looked at a small, round hole in the mattress.

"It looks to me," Inskip said, "as though someone had held a gun right up against the bottom of the mattress and pulled the trigger, holding the gun on an angle so the bullet wouldn't go all the way through."

"Well, let's find out," Mason told him.

"How are we going to do it?"

Mason pushed his finger in the hole, said, "That won't do it. Let's see if we can get something to use as a probe."

"There's a wire coat hanger in the closet," Inskip said. "I have a pair of pliers with wire cutters in my bag. I always carry pliers with me, because you never know what you're going to run up against in this business. Let me make a probe."

Inskip cut a piece of straight wire from a coat hanger while Mason held the mattress.

The detective ran the wire up inside the hole in the mattress for a few inches, then said, "Here it is. I can feel the wire hitting something hard."

"Can you make a hook on that wire and get it out?" Mason asked.

"I can try," Inskip said, "by putting a loop on the thing and working it over. I'll see what I can do."

Inskip used his pliers, then again put the wire probe in the hole in the mattress, manipulated it back and forth, up and down, said, "I think I've got it," then pulled. He pulled something back for a couple of inches, then the probe slipped loose.

"Have to get another hold," Inskip said. "I think I can widen that loop a little now."

He again worked on the wire, then once more pushed it up in the hole, said to Mason, "I've got it now." He pulled back on the wire. A metallic object popped out of the hole and fell down between the springs.

Inskip retrieved it. "A .38-caliber bullet," he said.

Mason stood motionless, his eyes half-slitted in thoughtful concentration.

"Well?" Inskip asked.

"Let's get the bed back into shape," Mason said. "Turn the mattress the way it was."

"Now what?" Inskip asked.

Mason said, "Take a sharp knife, take the pointed blade of the knife and make some kind of an identifying mark on that bullet so you can recognize it. Better put it on the base of the bullet. Try not to disfigure the bullet any more than possible."

"Then what?"

"Keep that bullet with you," Mason said. "Don't let it out of your possession at any time, no matter what happens."

"Now, wait a minute. *You'd* better keep it," Inskip said.

Mason shook his head. "I wouldn't want to be a witness in a case I was defending. I want you to keep that. And I want you to keep it with you. Don't let it out of your possession. Get some soft tissue and wrap it up so you don't destroy any of the striations on that bullet."

"Then what?" Inskip asked.

"Then," Mason said, "we make up the bed and you can go to sleep."

"But how the devil did that bullet get in that mattress?" Inskip asked.

"That," Mason said, "is one of the things we're going to have to find out."

"Do we want to tell anyone about this?"

"Not now," Mason said. "The police would laugh at us and claim we were faking evidence."

"Later on it'll be just that much worse," Inskip pointed out.

"I know," Mason told him. "That's why I want you to keep the bullet. What's your background? How long have you been in this business?"

"Quite a while. I was a deputy sheriff for a while, then I drifted up to Las Vegas, and worked there. I did some security work when Hoover Dam was going through. I've been with the government and now I'm working as a private operative."

"Ever been in trouble?"

"No."

"Nothing they can throw up at you? You're not vulnerable in any way?"

Inskip shook his he...

"All right," Mason t... nose is clean."
you can show it if you ha..., "save that wire probe so

"What's the significance ... "I don't know," Mason told... bullet?" Inskip asked.
"That is, I don't know
yet."

"Okay, you can call on me any...

"You going to tell the police abo... ...is?" Mason asked.
"I'd like to, Mr. Mason."

Mason said, "Hold it until ten o'clock ...ight, anyway. I
want first chance to tell the police about it. ...en you can—"

"Let's not talk time schedules," Inskip inte...upted. "Let's
leave it this way: I suggest to you that I thin... the police
should know about this, and you say that *you're* going to
tell them. Okay?"

"Okay," Mason said, "we'll leave it at that. I didn't say
when, did I?"

"No. You didn't say when. I told you to report to the po-
lice. You said you would. I assumed you meant right away.
However, because of that assumption I didn't pin you down.
That was my mistake. That's all it was, a mistake."

"A mistake," Mason agreed.

CHAPTER TWELVE

JUDGE CLINTON DEWITT nodded to Hamilton Burger. "Do
you wish to make an opening statement, Mr. Burger?"

Burger nodded, got up from the counsel table and lum-
bered over to the jury box.

"Ladies and gentlemen of the jury," he said, "I am going
to make one of the briefest opening statements I have ever

made. We expect to show that on the sixteenth day of October the defendant, Gerald Texas Global Development Corporation known as California usually referred to as Texas & Exploration Company was, prior to that day, was president of a corporation known as Texas Global.

"Mr. Conway was engaged in a proxy fight with a former official of the company, one Gifford Farrell. There were advertisements in the newspapers asking stockholders to send in proxies to a committee which was pledged to vote Mr. Farrell into power. That stockholders' meeting, ladies and gentlemen, is now three days away. At the insistence of the defendant, this case has been brought to trial so that the issues could be clarified before that meeting.

"We expect to show that the decedent, Rose M. Calvert, was employed by Gifford Farrell in a confidential capacity to make an ultrasecret list of the proxies which had been received. She typed out that list and gave it to Mr. Farrell.

"We expect to show that, in some way, the defendant found out the decedent was typing that list. When he found that he could not bribe her, he tried to take the list away from her at the point of a gun. She resisted and was shot.

"Thereupon, we expect to show that the defendant released to the press and gave to the police an utterly fantastic story designed to account for his presence in the room where the murder had been committed. We expect to show that the defendant went to his present attorney, Perry Mason, and consulted that astute lawyer, long before anyone knew a murder had been committed. We expect to show that Perry Mason immediately started working out what he hoped would be a good defense for the defendant.

"The defendant was spirited to the Gladedell Motel where he occupied Unit 21 during the night.

"We expect to show, at least by fair inference, that during that night the defendant went out and buried the weapon with which the crime had been committed.

"This was a Colt revolver No. 740818, being of .38 caliber and without any question, ladies and gentlemen of the jury, being the weapon that fired the bullet that took the life of Rose Calvert.

"We expect to show that the defendant went to the Redfern Hotel, entered the room where the murder was committed after giving the clerk a fictitious name so as to make the clerk believe that the young woman in the room was his secretary. We expect to show that the room where the murder was committed had been rented by the victim under this fictitious name. We expect to show, according to his own admission, that the defendant had a key to that room, that he entered that room, was there for an appreciable interval, and then left the room and went at once to consult an attorney. We will show that the defendant's attorney knew the identity of the murdered woman long before the police knew it, and that the only way he could have had this information was from the mouth of the defendant.

"Upon that evidence, ladies and gentlemen, we shall ask a verdict of first-degree murder."

Hamilton Burger turned and walked with ponderous dignity back to the counsel table.

Judge DeWitt glanced down at Perry Mason. "Does the defense wish to make an opening statement at this time, or do you wish to reserve your opening statement until later?"

Mason said, "I wish to make it at this time, Your Honor." He arose and walked over to stand in front of the jurors.

"May it please the Court and you ladies and gentlemen of the jury," Mason said, "I am going to make the shortest opening statement I have ever made in my life.

"The defendant is charged with first-degree murder. He is involved in a proxy fight for the control of the Texas Global, a corporation which has very large assets. We expect to show that an attempt was made to frame the defendant so that he would either be convicted of murder or in any event would be so discredited that it would be possible to wrest control of the corporation from him.

"In order to make a frame-up of this kind, ladies and gentlemen, it is necessary to use either one of two kinds of evidence, or to combine those two kinds of evidence: that is, perjured evidence or circumstantial evidence. We expect to show that both types of evidence were used in this case; that, under the law, wherever circumstantial evidence is relied upon by the prosecution, the Court will instruct you that, if the defense can advance any reasonable hypothesis other than that of guilt which will explain the circumstantial evidence, it is the sworn duty of the jurors to accept that hypothesis and acquit the defendant.

"You jurors have told us that you will abide by the instructions of the Court, and the Court will instruct you that that is the law.

"Under those circumstances, we shall expect a verdict of acquittal."

Mason turned and had started to walk back toward the counsel table when Hamilton Burger jumped to his feet.

"If the Court please," he said, "I feel that the jurors should be advised that it is incumbent upon the defense to offer a *reasonable* hypothesis. It has to appeal to the *reason,* to the sound common sense of the jurors."

"The Court will cover that matter in its instructions, Mr. District Attorney," the judge said. "Proceed with your case."

Hamilton Burger said, "My first witness will be Sgt. Holcomb."

Sgt. Holcomb came forward, was sworn and gave routine testimony as to the conversation with Perry Mason, going upstairs in the hotel, finding the body of a young woman sprawled out on the bed.

"Did you have some conversation with Mr. Mason as to how he happened to discover the body?" Burger asked.

"Yes."

"What did Mason say at that time?"

"Objected to as incompetent, irrelevant and immaterial," Mason said. "The conversation took place outside of the presence of the defendant."

"Did Mr. Mason admit to you that he was acting in his capacity as attorney for some client when he discovered the body?"

"He did."

"Did he say he was acting as attorney for this defendant?" Judge DeWitt asked.

"He didn't say so in so many words."

"The objection is sustained, at least for the present."

"You went up to Room 729?" Hamilton Burger asked.

"I did, yes, sir."

"What did you find?"

"I found the body of a young woman."

"Lying on the bed?"

"On the bed."

"She was dead?"

"She was dead."

"Can you describe the position of the body?"

"She was stretched out, half on her back, her right hand up in the air as though trying to protect herself and—"

"I move that part of the answer be stricken," Mason said, "as a conclusion of the witness."

"That will be stricken," Judge DeWitt said. "The witness can testify to the position of the hand, but cannot give his conclusion as to why the hand was in that position."

"Just indicate to the jury the position of the hand," Hamilton Burger said, smiling triumphantly, knowing that the point had reached the jurors regardless of the judge's ruling.

Sgt. Holcomb held up his hand.

"What time was this that you arrived at the hotel?" Burger asked.

"Approximately ten minutes to eight."

"And you went up almost immediately to the room?"

"Yes, sir."

"What time did you view the body?"

"I would say it was approximately eight o'clock. My notes show that I started looking around the suite at eight-four."

"Cross-examine," Hamilton Burger said abruptly.

"The right hand was held up above the face in the position you have indicated?" Mason asked.

"Yes."

"The left arm was hanging down?"

"Yes."

"Did you touch the body?"

"I touched the wrist to make sure there was no pulse."

"The wrist of which hand, the right or the left?"

"The right."

"You found no pulse?"

"No."

"The hand was held up in the position you have indicated?"

"Yes."

"It was not resting up against the face?"

"No, sir, it was not."

"There was a space between the back of the hand and the face?"

"There was."

"Yet the hand was up there and the woman was dead?"

"Certainly," Sgt. Holcomb snapped. "The condition was that known as *rigor mortis*."

"You know about *rigor mortis*?"

"Certainly."

"What is it?"

"It's what happens after a person is killed and the body stiffens."

"And the right hand was held up and *rigor mortis* had set in? Is that right?"

"Yes."

"Now, what about the left arm?"

"It was hanging over the side of the bed."

"Did you touch the left arm?"

"Yes, I touched the left arm."

"You say it was *hanging* down from the bed?"

"Yes."

"Do you mean by that that the left arm was not rigid?"

"It was hanging down. It was hanging from the shoulder."

"Did you move the left arm?"

"Slightly."

"You could move it?"

"Certainly."

"It was limp?"

"It was swinging from the shoulder. I didn't try to bend the elbow."

"But the arm was swinging from the shoulder, is that right?"

"Yes."

"Thank you," Mason said. "That's all. I have no further questions."

"My next witness will be Gifford Farrell," Hamilton Burger said.

Farrell had about him an air of hushed solemnity and grief as he walked quietly forward to the witness stand.

Some of the women jurors leaned forward to look at his lean, bronzed face. The men were more casual in their appraisal, but it was plain to be seen that the man's manner aroused interest.

Hamilton Burger turned the examination of Farrell over to his trial deputy, Marvin Elliott.

145

"Were you acquainted with Mrs. Norton Calvert during her lifetime?"

"I was."

"Her first name was Rose?"

"That is correct."

"She was married?"

"She was married and had separated from her husband."

"Do you know where Mrs. Calvert is now?"

"She is dead."

"Did you see her dead body?"

"I did."

"Where?"

"At the morgue."

"When?"

"On the seventeenth day of October of this year."

"Do you know what if anything Mrs. Calvert was doing at the time of her death?"

"She was working for me."

"In what capacity?"

"I am engaged in a proxy fight for control of Texas Global. I have done extensive advertising in the newspapers, and Mrs. Calvert was acting as my very confidential secretary, keeping tabs on the proxies which had come in."

Elliott turned to Perry Mason, said, "I show you a list containing the names of stockholders, the numbers of stock certificates, and a statement in regard to proxies which bears your initials and the initials of the defendant on each page. I believe you will stipulate this was a list which was turned over to the district attorney's office on the morning of October seventeenth."

"I will so stipulate. I will further stipulate that this was a paper which the defendant found under the front seat of his automobile late on the evening of October sixteenth. I will state further that we handed this list to the district attorney on the morning of October seventeenth with the statement that it might be evidence in the case, and the further statement that the defendant had no knowledge as to how or when it had been placed under the seat of his automobile."

"Very well," Elliott said, "we will stipulate as to the fact the defendant made this statement. We expect to disprove it."

Elliott turned to Farrell. "Mr. Farrell, I show you this list and ask you if you know what it is?"

"Yes, sir."

"What is it?"

"It is a list, dated the fourteenth of October, which purported to show the proxies that had been received to date."

"Who had possession of that list?"

"Rose Calvert."

"We ask that this list be received in evidence, Your Honor," Elliott said.

"Just a moment," Mason interposed. "I'd like to ask a few questions concerning this list before it is received in evidence."

"Very well," Judge DeWitt said.

Mason said, "My initials and the initials of the defendant are on that list. Is there any identifying mark of yours on that list?"

"No, sir, there is not."

"Then how do you know it is the same list which Rose Calvert had in her possession?"

Farrell's smile showed that he had been anticipating this question. "It is a completely phony list," he said. "It was purposely prepared and given to Rose Calvert, so that if anyone tried to force her to surrender the list she was making, she would have this phony list which was purposely misleading."

"That list did not reflect the true situation at that time?" Mason asked.

"It did not!"

"Who prepared that list?"

"It was prepared at my dictation."

"And you saw it in Rose Calvert's possession?"

"I did."

Mason turned to Judge DeWitt and said, "I think the statement that it was given Rose Calvert to be surrendered in case anyone tried to take the list from her is completely incompetent, irrelevant, and immaterial as far as this defendant is concerned. But because we are anxious to get at the truth of this case, we will not move to strike out that part of the answer. We have no objection to the list being placed in evidence."

"Very well," Judge DeWitt said, "it will be marked as the People's Exhibit and given the appropriate number by the clerk."

Marvin Elliott said, "I will now ask you, Mr. Farrell, if you gave Rose Calvert certain instructions on the sixteenth of October as to what she was to do at the Redfern Hotel?"

"Just a minute," Mason said. "I object on the ground that that is incompetent, irrelevant, and immaterial and not binding on the defendant. Unless it is shown that the defendant knew of this conversation or was present at the time it took place, it has no bearing on the case."

"It is part of the *res gestae*," Elliott said.

Judge DeWitt shook his head. "The objection is sustained."

Elliott said, "I have no further questions at this time."

Mason said, "That's all. I have no cross-examination."

Elliott said, "I'll call Robert Makon King."

Robert King walked quickly to the witness stand and took the oath.

"What is your occupation?" Elliott asked.

"I am a clerk at the Redfern Hotel."

"On the evening of October sixteenth did you have occasion to see a body in the hotel?"

"I did."

"Who showed you that body?"

"Sgt. Holcomb."

"Where was the body?"

"In Room 729."

"Were you able to identify that body?"

"Not by name, but as a guest in the hotel, yes."

"You had seen that young woman during her lifetime?"

"I had."

"Where and when?"

"She had entered the hotel and stated that she wanted a suite somewhere on the sixth or seventh floor, preferably the seventh. She stated that—"

"Never mind what she stated," Mason said. "I object on the ground that it's incompetent, irrelevant, and immaterial."

"This is very definitely part of the *res gestae*," Marvin Elliott said. "It accounts for certain facts which otherwise would be confusing."

"I think I will sustain the objection to the conversation," Judge DeWitt said. "You may ask what she did as part of the *res gestae*."

"Did she register for a room?"

"She did."

"Under what name?"

"Under the name of Gerald Boswell."

"I'm sorry," Elliott said, "that I can't ask you for the conversation. I will ask you if she paid for the suite in advance."

"She did. Yes, sir."

"You may cross-examine," Elliott said.

"Did this young woman have any baggage with her when she registered?" Mason asked.

"I didn't see any."

"Could there have been baggage which you didn't see?"

"It was the duty of the bellboy to take up the baggage."

"But she did pay for the suite in advance?"

"Yes, sir."

"And took it under the name of Gerald Boswell?"

"Yes, sir. She said he was her—"

"Just a minute," Judge DeWitt interrupted.

"Your Honor, I'm going to withdraw my objection to the conversation," Mason said. "I'm going to let the witness relate it."

"Very well," Judge DeWitt said.

King said, "She told me that she was the secretary of Gerald Boswell, that he wanted her to engage a suite for him, and that she would pay the rent in advance."

"Did she say she would do that because she had no baggage?" Mason asked.

"Now that you mention it, I believe she did."

"What time was this?"

"Sometime in the afternoon. I don't know just when. The records show it was just before two o'clock."

"What time did you come on duty?"

"At twelve o'clock in the afternoon."

"What time did you normally leave?"

"At eight o'clock in the evening."

Mason thought the situation over for a moment. "You're *certain* this was the young woman who rented the suite?"

"I'm certain."

"Your memory for faces is rather poor, isn't it?"

"On the contrary, it is very good."

"No further questions," Mason said.

"That's all," Elliott said. "I will wish to examine this witness upon another phase of the case later on in the trial."

"We object to the testimony being put on piecemeal," Mason said. "We feel that this witness should be interrogated at this time as to all the evidence which counsel intends to develop."

"Oh, Your Honor," Elliott said, "it would mean putting on our case out of order. We have to introduce an autopsy report, we have to introduce photographs."

"Well," Judge DeWitt said, "if counsel for the defense wants the evidence to be presented now, I think it would save time, at least, to ask the questions of this witness now."

"Very well," Elliott said. "Did you deliver an envelope to anyone who asked for messages in the name of Gerald Boswell on the evening of October sixteenth?"

"I did."

"To whom?"

"To the defendant."

"The gentleman sitting there next to Mr. Perry Mason?"

"Yes, sir."

"What time was that?"

"That was sometime around six-thirty. I can't give you the exact time."

"And did you have any further conversation with the defendant?"

"Not with the defendant. With his attorney and a gentleman with him, whom I have since learned was Paul Drake, a detective."

"And what was that conversation?"

"This detective, Mr. Drake, asked for messages for Gerald Boswell. I asked him for some identification and he showed me the key to Room 729. Then he went to the elevator."

"Carrying that key with him?"

"Yes."

"You don't know whether he went to Room 729?"

"Only by what he said afterward. He told me that he had."

"In the presence of Mr. Mason?"

"Yes, sir."

Mason said, "If the Court please, I am not objecting and because it is embarrassing for counsel to be a witness, I will stipulate that Mr. Drake and I went to the Redfern Hotel, that Mr. Drake asked for messages for Gerald Boswell, that he was told there were no messages, that he was asked for identification, that he produced a key to Room 729, that he went up to Room 729, that we discovered the body of this young woman on the bed, and that we notified police."

"Very well, that will simplify matters," Elliott said.

"Just a moment," Mason said. "I have a couple of questions on cross-examination.

"When Mr. Drake first asked for messages for Mr. Boswell, Mr. King, you told him that you had delivered a message to him earlier in the afternoon, didn't you?"

"Well, I was a little suspicious. I—"

"I'm not asking you whether you were suspicious. I'm asking you what you told him."

"Yes, I believe I told him something to that effect."

"Yet now you say it was the defendant to whom you delivered that message?"

"Well, I've had a chance to think it over."

"And to look at the defendant?"

"Yes."

"Yet on the sixteenth of October, when the occasion was more fresh in your mind, you stated to Paul Drake, the detective, that you had delivered the message to him. Did you not?"

"I may have said so, yes."

"And if you could have made a mistake in confusing Paul Drake with the defendant, isn't it possible that you could have made a mistake in regard to Rose Calvert and that it was some other young woman who rented the suite, 729?"

"No, sir. I am positive of my identification and I am not going to let you confuse me."

"Thank you," Mason said. "That's all!"

"Call Dr. K. C. Malone," Elliott said.

Dr. Malone came forward, was sworn, identified himself as Dr. Klenton C. Malone, an autopsy surgeon who had performed the autopsy on the body of Rose Calvert.

He testified as to the single bullet wound, the direction and nature of the wound, the fact that death was instantaneous, that there had been little external bleeding, that the wound was a contact wound, meaning that the gun had been held directly against the body when the wound was inflicted.

"When was the time of death?" Elliott asked.

"I fixed the time of death at between six-fifteen and seven o'clock on the evening of October sixteenth."

"Did you recover the fatal bullet?"

"I did."

"And what did you do with it?"

"I turned it over to Alexander Redfield, the ballistics expert."

"He was present when the autopsy was performed?"

"He was."

"Cross-examine," Elliott said to Perry Mason.

"When did you perform the autopsy?" Mason asked.

"It was the morning of the seventeenth."

"What time on the morning of the seventeenth?"

"About seven o'clock in the morning."

"Is that the time you usually go to work, Doctor?"

"No, sir. I was called to perform this autopsy by the district attorney. I was asked to perform it as early as possible."

"When were you called?"

"About ten o'clock in the evening."

"Why didn't you perform the autopsy that night?"

"There was not that much urgency about it. The district attorney wanted to have certain information by nine o'clock in the morning. I started the autopsy so I could give him the information he wanted."

"*Rigor mortis* had developed when the body was discovered?"

"I understand it had."

"When does rigor develop?"

"That is variable, depending upon several factors."

"Can you give me the approximate times during which rigor develops?" Mason asked.

"That I cannot," the witness said. "The authorities are in great dispute as to the development of rigor. Persons dying under conditions of excitement or emotion may develop rigor almost immediately. This is also true if death has been preceded by a physical struggle.

"I may state that there were conditions existing in this case which made it appear rigor had developed with considerable rapidity."

"Did you consider *rigor mortis* in connection with determining the time of death?"

"I did not. I determined the time of death from the contents of the stomach and intestines."

"Did you know when the last meal was ingested?"

"I was told that time could be fixed with great certainty. I know that death occurred approximately two hours after the last meal had been ingested."

"You were told when the meal was ingested?"

"Yes."

"That was hearsay?"

"It was the best information I was able to get."

"It was hearsay?"

"Naturally, Mr. Mason, I wasn't with this young woman when she took her lunch. I had to rely on what was told me."

"You didn't consider *rigor mortis* as an element in fixing the time of death?"

"I did not. There were indications that *rigor mortis* had set in almost immediately."

"What about post-mortem lividity?" Mason asked.

"The lividity had apparently just begun to develop. However, Mr. Mason, I didn't see the body at the time it was found. The deputy coroner made those observations."

"Now then," Mason said, "the wound in that body is as consistent with suicide as with murder, isn't it, Doctor?"

Dr. Malone hesitated, then finally said, "No, sir, it is not."

"Why?"

"From the position of the wound and the course of the bullet, it would have been virtually impossible for a right-handed woman to have held the weapon in exactly that position. And if the weapon was held in the left hand, the posture would have been cramped and somewhat unnatural. Moreover, Mr. Mason, we made chemical tests on the hands of the decedent to see if there was any indication a weapon had been held in the decedent's hand. There was none."

"You used the paraffin test?"

"Yes."

"Thank you," Mason said. "That's all."

Elliott called Dr. Reeves Garfield, who testified that he was from the coroner's office, that he had gone to the scene of the crime within an hour after the body had been discovered. He had supervised the taking of photographs, and had made on-the-spot observations. He had assisted in performing the autopsy. He gave it as his conclusion that death had taken place sometime between six-fifteen and seven o'clock.

"Cross-examine," Elliott said.

"The body was clothed when you saw it?"

"Yes."

"In rigor?"

"I will say this: It was partially in rigor."

"What do you mean by that?"

"*Rigor mortis* begins at the chin and throat muscles and slowly spreads downward until the entire body is involved.

Then rigor begins to leave the body in the same order in which it was formed."

"And rigor varies as to time?"

"Very much. Much more so than many of the authorities would indicate. A great deal depends upon individual circumstances. I have known of one case in which rigor developed almost immediately."

"What was the reason for that?"

"There had been a physical struggle, and an emotional disturbance at the time of death. I have known one other case where rigor was quite well developed within thirty minutes. And by that I mean a complete rigor."

"Under ordinary circumstances, the onset is much slower than that?"

"Oh, yes. Much slower."

"You say the body had developed *rigor mortis* at least in part. Were you there when the body was moved from the hotel?"

"Yes."

"And what was done with reference to rigor at that time?"

"The rigor was broken."

"What do you mean by that?"

"When a person dies," Dr. Garfield said, "the muscles are at first completely limp. The head can be moved from side to side with the greatest of ease. The limbs can be flexed. Then after a variable period of time, depending on circumstances, the rigor sets in, and when the rigor is completely developed, the body has become stiff."

"How stiff?"

"Very stiff indeed."

"Then what?"

"Then after a lapse of time as the muscles become alkaline again, the rigor leaves the body and the body once more becomes limp."

"Now, what do you mean by saying that rigor can be broken?"

"You can forcibly move the limbs after rigor has developed and, once the rigor is broken, it does not return."

Mason said, "Isn't it a fact, Doctor, that when you saw the body, there was rigor in the right arm, but that there was no rigor in the left arm?"

"I won't say that," Dr. Garfield said, "but I did notice that there was no rigor in the left shoulder."

"But there was in the right?"

"The right arm and shoulder were in complete rigor. The right hand was held up so that it was perhaps an inch or so from the face, but was stiff enough to remain in that position."

"Thank you, Doctor," Mason said. "Now I want to ask one more question: Isn't it a fact that it was possible for death to have taken place earlier in the afternoon?"

"Well . . ." Dr. Garfield hesitated.

"Go ahead," Mason said.

"There were certain conditions there that were puzzling. The development of the rigor, the post-mortem lividity, and a very faint discoloration of the left side of the body."

"What was this discoloration?"

"I am not certain. I would prefer not to discuss it because we finally came to the conclusion that it was not significant."

"But there was a discoloration?"

"Well, I wouldn't exactly call it a discoloration. It was just a faint tinge which was all but invisible except in certain lights. We decided, after discussing the matter, that it had no real significance. However, it had no significance because the contents of the stomach and intestines furnished a very accurate means of fixing the time of death."

"You personally examined the contents of the stomach and intestines?"

"Oh, yes."

"Can you determine when death occurred with reference to when the last meal was ingested?"

"I would say within a period of two hours to two hours and fifteen minutes."

"Then you think that this young woman had lunch at about four-thirty o'clock?"

"Apparently at exactly four-thirty."

"How do you know that?"

"Room Service sent lunch up to the room at four-thirty. Potatoes au gratin had been sent up by Room Service, and those remnants were found in the stomach. Roast turkey was sent up by Room Service, and those remnants were found in the stomach, as well as remnants of other items on the hotel's turkey plate luncheon."

"You have investigated this, of course?"

"Of course."

"And checked with Room Service in the hotel?"

"Yes."

"And what was your conclusion, Doctor?"

"As to the time of death?"

"As to the contents of the stomach."

"As compared with the lunch sent up?"

"Yes."

The witness hesitated.

"Well?" Mason asked.

"It is hard to answer that question without bringing in hearsay evidence," Dr. Garfield said. "The hotel restaurant was able to check the order sent out—a regular plate dinner of roast turkey with dressing. The decedent also ordered asparagus. We found all those articles in the stomach."

"Any other articles?" Mason asked.

"Yes."

"What?"

"Green peas."

"But there were no green peas on the luncheon sent up?" Mason asked. "Those peas must have come from another source?"

"There *were* green peas on the luncheon," Dr. Garfield said positively. "The hotel records show no peas listed on the check, but they were sent up. They had to be on that lunch tray. The hotel employees all admitted it was very possible the records were in error and the peas simply had not been put on the bill because of an oversight."

"Did she sign the check for Room Service?"

"No, sir, she paid it in cash."

Elliott said, "We expect to show the contents of the last meal which was sent up by Room Service, and we expect to show that green peas were added by an inexperienced waiter who neglected to put them on the bill. There can be no question as to what actually happened."

"If the Court please," Mason said, "I take exception to the statement by counsel that there can be no question as to what happened. Counsel is advancing his own conclusions."

"I was merely trying to shorten the cross-examination of this witness, save the time of the Court, and keep from confusing the issues in the minds of the jury," Elliott said.

Judge DeWitt said, "Just a moment, gentlemen. Despite the short time spent in getting a jury, it has reached the hour for the afternoon adjournment. Court will take a recess until ten o'clock tomorrow morning. In the meantime, the jurors are instructed not to discuss this case with anyone or permit it to be discussed in their presence, nor to form or express any opinion concerning the matter until it is finally submitted for their consideration. I have previously admonished the jury on this point and I think they understand their duties. Court will recess until ten o'clock tomorrow morning.

"The defendant is remanded to custody."

Mason turned to smile reassuringly at Conway. "I think we've got them, Jerry," he said.

Conway said, "I don't see how you figure it. I think we're licked."

"What do you mean?"

Conway said, "Our only hope was in getting Giff Farrell to show himself in his true light before the jurors. He came off with flying colors."

Mason grinned. "You mean I didn't cross-examine him vigorously enough?"

Conway said, "You're running the show, Mason. But you must be able to see for yourself what has happened. Farrell's testimony is now completely established and he hasn't even been embarrassed. Why didn't you ask him about his relations with the dead woman, about those photographs?"

"Because," Mason said, "if we ever get that far, I am going to force the district attorney to put Gifford Farrell on in rebuttal, and by that time I'm going to have him sketched as quite a villain. When I get done with him then, he's going to be an entirely different individual from the debonair man who occupied the witness stand this afternoon."

"Well, I hope so," Conway said. "However, one thing is certain. I've completely lost control of Texas Global."

Mason patted him on the shoulder. "Take it easy, Conway," he said. "And remember people are watching you in the courtroom. Don't act discouraged. Act as though you felt certain right would triumph."

"You can't smile in a situation like that," Conway said. "The bottom has dropped out, and—"

"Don't grin," Mason said, "simply look less overwhelmed."

Conway straightened himself, gave Mason a smile.

Mason clapped him on the back, said in a loud voice,

"Okay. See you tomorrow. And by tomorrow night you should be out. Sleep tight."

Mason picked up his brief case and left the courtroom.

CHAPTER THIRTEEN

MASON, PAUL DRAKE, and Della Street were gathered in the lawyer's office.

Mason said, "What's new with Farrell, Paul?"

"Not a damned thing," Drake said. "He's keeping his nose so clean it shines."

Mason frowned and said, "Now look, Paul, whoever did this job *had* to have a female accomplice. She was rather young, good-looking, with a sexy figure that she wasn't averse to showing.

"This woman who left the hotel must have been the woman that Conway saw in Room 729. That's the woman who held the gun on him, who really holds the key to the whole plot.

"Now, Farrell has put himself entirely in the power of this woman. She must be someone who's infatuated with him. Farrell wouldn't dare let her be where she could cool off as far as he's concerned. He wouldn't dare let her conscience start bothering her. He *must* be seeing her."

"But he isn't," Drake said. "Farrell has been 100 per cent circumspect. He has hardly gone out socially since this case came up. Apparently, he was pretty much broken up by the death of Rose Calvert. He must have been pretty much attached to her."

"Phooey!" Mason said. "He's seeing this other woman somewhere. . . . It must be one of the girls in his office."

"We've got a line on every girl in his office," Drake said. "I've got a pile of stuff two feet thick, Perry. I can tell you so much about those girls that it would frighten them if they knew we knew it. One of them is married and living with her husband. One of them is engaged. One of them is going steady. The other is a good-looking babe that Farrell has been out with once or twice, but she's a girl who's built for speed, narrow hips and a light chassis. There's another one that Farrell probably had an affair with at one time, but she's a tall babe, one of these long, willowy gals.

"Conway says this woman who emerged from the bedroom and then held the gun on him had a figure and was of average height. . . . Don't worry, if Farrell starts trying to keep any female accomplice in line, we'll spot her."

"He'll have to do it when the case gets a little hotter," Mason said.

"How's it going, Perry?"

Mason said, "Well, I'm getting my theory worked into the case so unobtrusively that the prosecution doesn't even know it's there. Tomorrow I'll spring it."

"Your theory that the body was moved?"

"That's right," Mason said. "The body had lain on its left side. There had been just the start of that peculiar discoloration which is known as post-mortem lividity. *Rigor mortis* had probably set in rather soon. The right hand and right arm were doubled up and probably the left arm was sticking straight out. When the body was moved and placed on that bed, it was necessary for whoever did it to break the *rigor mortis* in the left shoulder so the arm would hang down somewhat naturally. If that left arm had been sticking out straight as a poker, it would have been a dead giveaway and anyone would have known that the body had been moved. With the body lying on the bed, it became necessary for that left arm to be hanging down. So rigor was broken at the shoulder.

"That Bob King is a miserable liar. He's trying to bolster up the prosecution's case, but he's not doing a good job of it.

"How are you coming along with your elevator girl, Paul?"

"Swell!" Drake said grinning. "That's one of the best assignments I ever had. She's a darned good scout, Perry, and is fun to be with, although at times I do wish she'd quit that everlasting gum chewing."

"What have you found out from her?"

"I've found out all she knows. I can tell you enough stuff about the operation of the Redfern Hotel to make your hair curl. I can tell you things about the bell captains, about the clerks—and I can tell you this: The woman who went up to Room 729 definitely didn't have any baggage, and that's the reason she paid in advance.

"My elevator girl says that the bell captain was grumbling. He thought that the girl intended to muscle in on his racket, and he was determined that, if she started entertaining men in the room, he'd have her thrown out unless she decorated the mahogany with a cut."

Mason paced the floor. "There's something funny there, Paul. The position of the body on the bed was changed. Now, why would it be changed? Why did someone discharge a gun into the mattress in Room 728? The gun was pushed up against the mattress so it wouldn't make any loud noise.

"The noise made by a contact wound when a gun is held up against a body or when the gun is pushed up against a mattress of that sort isn't loud enough to attract attention. It's not much louder than exploding a paper bag."

"But why change the position of the body?" Drake asked. "Why juggle guns?"

"That," Mason said, "is something we're going to have to find out. Beginning tomorrow, I'm going to start getting some of this stuff in front of the jury, and then I'm going to needle the prosecution by asking it these questions. I'm going to start punching holes in the prosecution's theory of the case."

"Enough to get an acquittal for Conway?"

"I think so," Mason said. "I'm not worried so much about that as I am that the public may take it as a Scotch verdict: guilty but not proven, and Conway will never be able to live it down."

"He's not the kind who would try very hard," Drake said.

"In some ways he's not a fighter," Mason admitted. "He gets discouraged and throws in the sponge. He'll fight like the devil on a business deal, but in a matter of this sort which affects his personal integrity, he feels completely crushed.

"You keep in touch with your elevator operator—what the devil's her name?"

"Myrtle Lamar," Drake said.

"She isn't taking you seriously, is she?" Della Street asked. "You aren't going to wind up breaking her heart, are you, Paul?"

"Not Myrtle!" Drake said, grinning. "Her heart is made of India rubber."

"Those are the kinds that fool you," Della Street said. "Probably beneath that cynical exterior, she's extremely sensitive and— Don't you go destroying her illusions, Paul Drake!"

"You can't destroy them," Drake said, "because she hasn't got 'em. As a matter of fact, I get a kick out of being with her. She knows that I'm trying to pick her brains to find out something about the case that has eluded us so far, and she's doing everything she can to help. She's telling me every little thing she can think of about the operation of the hotel, about what happened that night and all that.

"My gosh! The gossip I can tell you about the things that

go on in that hotel! And what a miserable little stooge this Bob King is! He'd do absolutely anything just to curry favor with the authorities."

Again Mason started pacing the floor. "The trouble is we're one woman short in this matter. That woman couldn't have disappeared into thin air. She couldn't have disappeared from Gifford Farrell's life. He wouldn't have let her.

"Tomorrow I'm going to start asking embarrassing questions. The prosecution isn't accustomed to trying cases against lawyers who know anything about forensic medicine. The average lawyer considers it out of his line, and doesn't bother to study up on it. In this case the medical testimony is of the greatest importance and has some peculiar angles.

"Moreover, we're missing that woman and—"

Suddenly Mason stopped stock-still in his pacing, paused in the middle of a sentence.

Della Street looked up quickly. "What is it, Chief?"

Mason didn't answer her question for a matter of two or three seconds, then he said slowly, "You know, Paul, in investigative work the worst thing you can do is to get a theory and then start trying to fit the facts to it. You should keep an open mind and reach your conclusion after the facts are all in."

"Well," Drake said, "what's wrong?"

"Throughout this entire case," Mason said, "I've let my thinking be influenced by Jerry Conway. He's told me that this was a frame-up which was engineered by Gifford Farrell, that the line to his office had been tapped, and that he was suckered into this thing by Farrell."

"Well, it stands to reason," Drake said. "We know that someone cut in on the program Evangeline Farrell had mapped out for Conway. Mrs. Farrell was going to make certain that he wasn't followed and then she was going to have him meet her where she could give him those papers.

"She was to call him at six-fifteen, but somebody beat her to the punch by a couple of minutes and—"

"And we've jumped to the conclusion that it was some accomplice of Giff Farrell!" Mason said.

"Well, why not? The whole setup, the substitution of guns, the burying of the fatal weapon—all that shows a diabolical ingenuity and—"

Mason said, "Paul, I've got an idea. Get your friend Myrtle Lamar and have her in court tomorrow. Sit there in court and have her listen. I want to have her beside you."

"She has to work, Perry. . . ."

"I'll serve a subpoena on her as a witness for the defense," Mason said. "Then she'll have to be there. I'm beginning to get the nucleus of an idea, Paul.

"You say you've had trouble holding your man Inskip in line?"

"I told you we'd have trouble," Drake said. "He keeps feeling that he's withholding evidence that the police should have, and it bothers him. When you finally spring your idea and he's called as a witness, the police will want to know why he didn't give them the tip, and—"

"Let him give them the tip," Mason said.

"What do you mean?"

"Get hold of Inskip," Mason said. "Tell him to go to the police. Let him tell the police that his conscience is bothering him and he can't hold out any longer, that he knows I have an ace in the hole, that we discovered this hole in the mattress in Room 728. Let him give them the bullet that we took from the mattress and let Redfield check that bullet with the Smith & Wesson gun Conway turned over to the police. The bullets will check."

Drake said, "That would be awfully nice from Inskip's viewpoint but it would leave you right out in the open,

Perry. They would know exactly what you were trying to do."

"That's okay," Mason said. "That suits my plans fine!"

"And then what'll happen?"

"Then tomorrow," Mason said, "the prosecution will feel they know what I'm leading up to and they'll want time to combat it. I think this Dr. Garfield is a pretty fair sort of individual. I'll start laying the foundation, and Hamilton Burger will go into a panic. He'll start stalling for time."

"But you've been the one who wanted to rush things along so you could have the case over before the stockholders'—"

"I know, I know," Mason interrupted. "There's still time. Go ring up Inskip. Tell him to go tell the police the whole story!"

"The whole story?" Drake said.

"Everything!" Mason said. "Then get your girl, Myrtle Lamar, and be in court tomorrow morning. I'm beginning to get the damnedest idea and I think it's predicated on sound logic."

CHAPTER FOURTEEN

JUDGE DEWITT SAID, "The jurors are all present. The defendant is in court. At the conclusion of yesterday's testimony Dr. Reeves Garfield was on the stand. Will you please resume your place on the stand, Dr. Garfield?"

Dr. Garfield took his place in the witness chair.

"Directing your attention to this discoloration which you noticed on the left side of the body," Mason asked, "can you tell us more about the nature of that discoloration?"

"It was barely noticeable; only in certain lights could you see it. It was simply a very, very faint change in the complexion of the skin."

"Would you say that it had no medical significance, Doctor?"

"I would never state that any phenomenon one may find in a cadaver in a murder case had no medical significance."

"Was there a dispute as to whether this color had any *real* significance or not?"

Hamilton Burger was on his feet. "Your Honor, we object to that as being improper cross-examination. It calls for something which is incompetent, irrelevant, and immaterial. It makes no difference whether there was a dispute or not. This Court is trying this defendant not for the purpose of determining what argument someone may have had, but for the purpose of getting the ultimate facts."

"I will sustain the objection," Judge DeWitt said.

"Was there a dispute between you and Dr. Malone as to the significance of this slight discoloration?"

"Same objection," Hamilton Burger said.

Judge DeWitt hesitated for a long, thoughtful moment, then said, "The same ruling. I will sustain the objection."

"Isn't it a fact," Mason said, "that this slight discoloration may have been due to the fact that the body lay for some appreciable interval after death on its left side, and that the slight discoloration marked the beginnings of a post-mortem lividity, which remained after the body had again been moved?"

"That is, of course, a possibility."

"A distinct possibility?"

"Well, it is a possibility. I will concede that."

"Now, did you ever know of a case where there had been a pronounced development of *rigor mortis* in the right arm and shoulder with no *rigor mortis* in the left shoulder, unless someone had broken the rigor?"

"I know of no such case."

"Is it your opinion that the rigor in the left shoulder had been broken?"

The witness shifted his position on the witness stand, looked somewhat hopelessly at Hamilton Burger.

"That's objected to," Hamilton Burger said, "on the ground that the question is argumentative, that it calls for a conclusion of the witness."

"The objection is overruled," Judge DeWitt said. "The witness is an expert, and is testifying as to his opinion. Answer the question."

Dr. Garfield said slowly, "It is *my* opinion that the rigor had been broken."

"And it is your opinion that the position of the body had been changed after death, and prior to the time you saw it there in Room 729 at the Redfern Hotel?"

There was a long period of hesitation, then Dr. Garfield said reluctantly, "That is my opinion."

"Thank you," Mason said. "That is all."

"No further questions," Elliott announced.

Hamilton Burger seemed preoccupied and worried. He bent over and whispered something to his trial deputy, and then ponderously tiptoed from the courtroom.

Elliott said, "My next witness will be Lt. Tragg."

Tragg came forward and was sworn. He testified in a leisurely manner that was hardly in keeping with Tragg's usually crisp, incisive manner on the stand.

He had, he said, attended a conference of officers on October seventeenth. The defendant had appeared. With him had appeared his attorney, Perry Mason.

"Did the defendant make a statement?"

"Yes."

"Was the statement free and voluntary?"

"It was."

Elliott asked him to describe what was said.

Slowly, almost tediously, Tragg repeated the conversation in detail, with Elliott glancing at his watch from time to time.

The morning recess was taken and Court reconvened. Tragg's testimony was still dragging on until at eleven-thirty he was finished.

"You may cross-examine," Elliott said.

"No questions," Mason said.

Elliott bit his lip.

His next witness was the uniformed officer who had sat in on the conference in the district attorney's office. The uniformed officer was still giving his testimony about what had happened when Court took its noon adjournment.

"What's happening?" Conway whispered. "They seem to be bogging down."

"They're worried," Mason whispered back. "Just keep a stiff upper lip."

The jurors filed out of the courtroom. Mason walked over to where Paul Drake, Della Street, and Myrtle Lamar, the elevator operator, were standing talking.

Myrtle Lamar shifted her wad of gum, grinned at Mason. "Hello, big boy," she said.

"How's everything?" Mason asked.

"Sort of tedious this morning," she said. "Why the subpoena? I'm supposed to be on duty tonight and I should be getting my beauty sleep."

"You don't need it," Mason told her.

"I will before I get done."

Drake put his hand on her arm. "We'll take care of you all right. Don't worry!"

"You don't know the manager up there at the Redfern Hotel. Women must have made a habit of turning him down. He loves to kick them around. He'd throw me out on my ear as easy as he'd snap a bread crumb off the table."

"You don't snap bread crumbs. You remove them with a little silver scoop," Drake said.

"You and your damned culture," she said.

"Come on," Mason told her. "We're going out."

"Where?"

"We're going visiting."

"My face," she said, "has bad habits. It needs to be fed."

"We'll get it fed," Mason said.

"Okay, that's a promise!"

Mason shepherded them down in the elevator into his car, drove carefully but skillfully.

"Where?" Drake asked.

Mason looked at his watch. "Not far."

Mason stopped the car in front of an apartment house, went to the room telephones, called Evangeline Farrell.

When her voice came on the line, the lawyer said, "Mrs. Farrell, I want to see you at once on a matter of considerable importance."

"I'm not dressed for company," she said.

"Put on something," Mason told her. "I have to be back in court and I'm coming up."

"Is it important?"

"Very!"

"It concerns the case?"

"Yes."

"Come on up," she told him.

Mason nodded to the others. They took the elevator.

Mrs. Farrell opened the apartment door, then fell back in surprise, clutching at the sheer negligee.

"You didn't tell me anyone was with you," she said.

"I'm sorry," Mason told her. "I overlooked it, perhaps. I'm in a terrible hurry. I have to be back in court at two o'clock."

"But what in the world—?"

Mason said, "You could buy us a drink. This is important."

She hesitated for a long moment, then said, "Very well."

"May I help you?" Della Street asked.

"Oh, I'm sorry," Mason said. "I haven't introduced these people to you."

Mason performed introductions, mentioning only names except for Della Street. "My confidential secretary," he explained.

"Come on," Della Street said, "I'll help you."

Somewhat hesitantly Mrs. Farrell moved toward the kitchenette. When she had gone, Mason said to the elevator operator, "Have you ever seen her before?"

"I think I have. If I could get a better look at her feet, I'd be sure. I'd like to see her shoes."

"Let's look," Mason said. He walked boldly to the bedroom door, opened it, beckoned to Paul Drake who took Myrtle's arm, led her along into the bedroom.

The elevator operator tried to hang back, but Drake shifted his arm around her waist.

"Know what you're doing, Perry?" Drake asked, as Mason crossed the bedroom.

"No," Mason said, "but I have a hunch." He opened a closet door.

"Take a look at the shoes, Myrtle," Mason said. "Do they mean anything to you? Wait a moment! I guess we don't need those. Take a look at this." The lawyer reached back into the closet, pulled out a suitcase. It had the initials "R. C."

"Just what do you think you're doing?" an angry, icy voice demanded.

Mason turned, said, "Right at the moment, I'm checking the baggage that you removed from the Redfern Hotel, Mrs. Farrell, and this young woman who is the elevator operator who was on duty the day of the murder is looking at your shoes to see if she recognizes the pair you wore. She has the peculiar habit of noticing people's feet."

Mrs. Farrell started indignantly toward them, then suddenly stopped in her tracks.

Mason said, "Let's take a look inside that suitcase, Paul."

"You can't do that," she said. "You have no right."

"Okay," Mason said, "if you want it the hard way, we'll do it the hard way. Go to the phone, Paul. Call Homicide and ask them to send up some officers with a warrant. We'll stay here until they arrive."

Evangeline Farrell stood looking at them with eyes that held an expression of sickened dismay.

"Or perhaps," Mason said, "you'd like to tell us about it. We haven't very much time, Mrs. Farrell."

"Tell you about what?" she asked, trying to get hold of herself.

"About renting Room 729 and saying you were the secretary of Gerald Boswell, and that he was to occupy the room for the night.

"Tell us about shooting Rose Calvert, who was in 728; about sitting there waiting, trying to figure out what you'd do, then taking the body across the hall. . . . Did you manage that alone? Or did someone help you?"

She said, "You can't do that to me. You— I don't know what you're talking about."

Mason walked over to the telephone, picked up the receiver, said to the operator, "I want Lt. Tragg at—"

"Wait!" Mrs. Farrell screamed at him. "Wait! You've got to help me."

Mason said into the mouthpiece of the telephone, "Never mind." He dropped the phone into its cradle.

"All right," she said. "All right! I'll tell you. I'll tell you the whole story. I've been frightened stiff ever since it happened. But I didn't kill her. I didn't! Please, please believe that I didn't kill her."

"Who did?" Mason asked.

"Gifford," she said.

"How do you know?"

"He must have. He's the only one. He thought she was selling out. I guess he must have followed me to the hotel. He knew I was there."

"Go on," Mason said. "You only have a minute or two. Get it off your chest. What happened?"

She said, "I wanted to give Mr. Conway the lists of stockholders who had sent in proxies. I wanted to do it under such circumstances that Gifford would think his little mistress had sold him out. She was at the Redfern Hotel. She had this room in 728. She was typing. You could hear her through the transom banging away on a portable typewriter like mad. I told you the truth about getting the used carbon paper."

"Why did you do all this?" Mason asked. "Why did you rent that suite?"

"I didn't want Jerry Conway to lose control of Texas Global."

"Why?" Mason asked. "I would think your interests would have been elsewhere. I would think that your only hope of getting money out of your husband depended upon letting him get in the saddle by—"

"I had to look at it two ways," she interrupted. "I've already told you. I felt that under Conway's management my Texas Global stock would be valuable. I wasn't so sure about Gifford's management. I figured that by the time this tramp he was running around with got hers, and when the next tramp he would be running around with got *hers,* my stock would be worthless."

"All right," Mason said, "what did you do?"

She said, "I knew that my husband was playing around with Rose Calvert. I followed her to the hotel. She registered as Ruth Culver."

Mason's voice showed excitement. "Had she registered that way before?"

"Yes. In two hotels."

"I want the names of those hotels," Mason said.

"I can give you the names, the dates and the room numbers.

"While she was at those other hotels, my husband was bringing her data, and she was typing out lists of proxy holders on her portable typewriter. Then one day she left a copy of the list in her car. The car was parked, and the doors weren't even locked. I realize now it was a trap. I didn't know it at the time. I reached in and got this list. That, of course, was a completely phony list that they were hoping would lull Conway into a sense of security. I walked right into that trap."

"Go on," Mason said.

"I wanted Conway to have that list, but I didn't want him to know where it came from. So I telephoned him, and disguised my voice. I told him to remember me by the name of Rosalind."

"You told him a lot of things about being followed by detectives and goon squads?" Mason asked. "Why was that?"

"That was just to protect my identity and make him cautious."

"Actually you didn't know he was followed?"

"I didn't *think* he was. This Gashouse Baker was entirely a figment of my imagination."

"All right. Go ahead. What happened?"

"Well, I decided I'd do a little amateur detective work. I thought I'd get down to where I could follow Rose Calvert from her apartment. I wanted to know exactly what she was doing and where she was going.

"On the morning of the sixteenth, she went to the Redfern Hotel and registered as Ruth Culver. She was given Room 728.

"Once or twice during the morning, I went up in the elevator and walked down the corridor. I could hear her pounding away like mad on her typewriter. She stopped once around twelve-thirty when Room Service brought her lunch.

"You see, I had all the advantage because I knew what she looked like, but she didn't know me when she saw me. I was just a complete stranger as far as she was concerned. I had pictures of her in a Bikini bathing suit. I had pictures of her in the nude. I had followed my husband to her apartment. I knew all about her, and she knew nothing about me."

"What happened at the hotel?" Mason asked, looking at his watch impatiently.

"Well, about ten minutes to two, I guess it was, Rose came downstairs and went out. She tossed her key on the counter for the clerk to put away. The clerk was busy, and when he had his back turned, I just walked up and took the key to room 728. And then just after I'd picked it up and before I could turn away from the counter, the clerk turned around and came toward the counter and asked me if there was something I wanted. Then was when I had a brilliant inspiration. I told him that I was a secretary for Gerald Boswell, that Gerald Boswell had some work he wanted done, and had asked me to get a suite in his name. I told him that, since I didn't have any baggage, I would pay the price of the suite and Mr. Boswell would move in sometime that evening. I asked him if he would give me two keys to the suite, so that I could get in and so I could give one to Mr. Boswell.

"The clerk didn't think anything of it. I suppose he may have thought it was a date with a married woman sneaking away to meet her lover, but things like that don't even cause a lifted eyebrow in that hotel—not from what I hear."

"Go on," Mason said. "Never mind the hotel. We want to know what you did."

"Well, I told the clerk I wanted something not too low down and not too high up, something around the seventh floor. He said he had 729 vacant and I took that. I didn't have any baggage so there was nothing to take up to the room. I took the key, and after a while I walked up and settled down to listen. My room was right across the corridor from 728. I left the door slightly open and sat there watching.

"About two-thirty Rose Calvert came back."

"But you had her key?"

"Yes, but you know how those things are. Keys are always getting lost around a hotel. They have several keys for each room, and sometimes the clerk will put one in the wrong box, or a tenant will walk away with it, so they always have duplicates. I don't suppose Rose had any trouble whatever getting a key to the room. She simply said she'd left hers at the desk, and the clerk dug one out for her."

"Then what happened?"

"Well, then she didn't do any more typing, and I began to realize that probably the list I had was either obsolete or else a completely phony list they wanted to use as a red herring."

"So what did you do?"

"So I went down and telephoned Mr. Conway. I took the name of Rosalind, and gave him the old rigmarole."

"You didn't call from the room?"

"No, I didn't even call from the hotel. I walked a couple of blocks to a phone booth and phoned from there."

"Go ahead," Mason said.

"Well, I went down and put in this telephone call, then I went shopping for a few things. Then I phoned again and went back to the room."

"Then what?"

"Well, I started watching again."

"Now, wait a minute," Mason said. "Let's fix this time schedule. You were in your room at two-thirty?"

"That's right."

"Rose Calvert was back in her room by that time?"

"Yes. That's when she came in."

"Then you went out to telephone Conway?"

"Yes, twice. In between I walked around a little while getting some fresh air and doing some shopping."

"What time did you get back?"

"I didn't look at my watch."

"All right, go on. What happened?"

"Well, I sat by the door listening for a while, but couldn't hear anything. Then along about three-thirty I was in the bathroom. That was when I heard a peculiar sound which I thought was made by someone banging on my bedroom door.

"I was completely paralyzed with fright. It was as though someone had given my door a good, hard kick. I felt certain someone had discovered that I was spying on Rose Calvert across the hall, and I didn't know what to do for a moment.

"So I went to the door of the suite, put on my most innocent expression and opened it. No one was there. I looked up and down the corridor. I can't begin to tell you how relieved I felt. Then just as I was closing the door, having it opened just a crack, I saw the door across the corridor start to open. So I glued my eye to the door and . . . and—"

"Go on," Mason said, his voice showing his excitement. "What happened?"

"Gifford walked out."

"Gifford Farrell, your husband?"

She nodded.

"Go on," Mason said. "Then what?"

"I didn't think anything of it at the time, because he'd been calling on her when she had rooms in the other hotels. I don't think there was anything romantic about *those* calls. She had her portable typewriter with her, and I guess she was doing typing work, and they took all those precautions to keep anyone from knowing what was going on."

"Go on," Mason said. "What happened?"

"Well, I closed my door tight and waited awhile, then I opened it awhile and listened, but there were no more sounds coming from the room across the hall.

"And then suddenly I began to wonder if Rose might not have gone out while I was out. I went downstairs and out to the phone booth, called the Redfern Hotel and asked to be connected with Room 728."

"What happened?"

"I could hear the noise the line makes when there's a phone ringing and there is no answer. The operator told me my party was out and asked if I wanted her paged."

"I said no, that I'd call later."

"And then?" Mason asked.

"Then, I went back in a hurry, took the elevator up to the seventh floor, and tapped gently on 728. When there was no answer, I used my key and opened the door."

"What did you find?"

"Rose Calvert was lying there dead on the bed. And then suddenly I realized what that noise had been. My husband had shot her and he'd shot her with my gun."

"What do you mean, your gun?"

"My gun. It was lying there on the floor by the bed."

"Your gun?"

"Mine," she said. "I recognized it. It was one that the Texas Global had bought for the cashier to carry because the cashier lived out in the country. He was afraid to drive alone at night for fear someone would try to hold him up and get the combination of the safe. I guess he was getting a little nervous and neurotic. He died a few months afterward.

"Anyway, the company bought him the gun, and after he died, Gifford took the gun and gave it to me."

"You recognized the gun?"

"Yes."

"How?"

"I used to sleep with it under my pillow. I dropped it once, and there was a little nick out of the hard, rubber handle. Then once I'd got some fingernail enamel on it and there was just that little spot of red.

"Of course, I'd never have noticed it if I hadn't seen Gifford leave the room. Knowing he'd shot her, I suddenly wondered about the weapon. And then I knew it was my weapon."

"How long had he had it?"

"I moved out on him, and like a fool I didn't take the gun with me. So it was there in the apartment. . . ."

"I see," Mason said. "What did you do?"

"Well, I decided to leave things just the way they were and quietly check out of the hotel, so I opened the door and started out into the corridor, and that was when I got trapped."

"What do you mean?"

"The chambermaid was walking by just as I opened the door, and she looked at me, then suddenly did a double take and said, 'Is *that* your room?' "

"What did you do?"

"I had to brazen it through. She evidently had been talking with Rose, and knew that that wasn't my room."

"Well," Mason said, "what did you do?"

"I thought fast. I told her no, that it wasn't my room, that it was my friend's room, and that she'd given me her key and asked me to go and wait for her, but that I couldn't wait any longer. I was going downstairs and leave a note for her."

"Did you convince the chambermaid?"

"That's the trouble. I didn't. The chambermaid kept staring at me, and I know she thought I was a hotel thief. But she didn't say anything. Probably she was afraid of getting into trouble. That trapped me. I knew that the minute the body of Rose Calvert was found in that room, I'd be connected with the crime. I was in a panic. I walked down the corridor to the elevator, waited until the chambermaid had gone into another room, and then I walked back to 729, let myself in and sat there in a complete blue funk. I didn't know what the devil to do."

"What did you do?"

"After a while I got the idea that I wanted. I couldn't afford to let Rose Calvert's body be found in 728, but if I could move the body over to 729 and then check out of 728 under the name of Ruth Culver, which was the name she had registered under, everything would be all right. If her body was found in 728, the chambermaid would have remembered all about my leaving the place, and given a description of me. Later on she'd have been able to recognize me. Of course, I knew police could trace the gun. But if I could have it appear that nothing unusual had happened in 728, but that the person who was murdered was the one who had checked in at 729, *then* I would be sending everybody off on a completely false trail."

"Go on," Mason said. "What did you do?"

"I did some fast thinking. I wanted to make it appear that the crime had taken place much later than had actually been the case. I waited until I was certain the corridor was clear, then I hurried across and started packing all the baggage in the room. Rose had been using her portable typewriter and there were a lot of fresh carbon papers dropped into the wastebasket. I picked those up, and that was when I realized I had a very complete list of the work she had been doing. She had been making a whole lot of copies, and had used fresh carbon paper. I took the sheets of used carbon paper with me."

"Go on," Mason said.

"Then I went back to Room 729, telephoned Room Service and asked them what they had for lunch.

"They said it was pretty late for lunch, and I told them I needed something to eat and asked them what they had. They said they could fix me a roast turkey plate, and I told them to bring it up.

"The waiter brought it up, and I paid him in cash, and gave him a good tip so he'd remember me. But I kept my face averted as much as possible.

"Then I ate the dinner and asked him to come up for the dishes."

"And then?"

"And then, all of a sudden, I realized that Jerry Conway was going to start out to get that list."

"Go on."

"Originally, I'd intended to telephone him at the drugstore, and tell him to go and ask for a message which had been left for him at a certain hotel. So suddenly I realized that it might be possible to kill two birds with one stone, and really to pull something artistic."

"So?" Mason asked.

"So," she said, "after I called Room Service, I had the waiter come and take the dishes, and then I went down to the drugstore and bought a jar of this prepared black mud that women put on their faces for massages. It spreads smoothly over the face and then, when it dries, it pulls the skin. The general idea is that it smooths out wrinkles and eliminates impurities from the skin and all that. It has an astringent effect and pulls the facial muscles. I knew it would make my face completely unrecognizable."

"So you put that mud on?" Mason asked.

She nodded, said, "I called up the pay station at the drugstore from the booth in the hotel, and I was even smart enough to call up a few minutes before six-fifteen so that it would look as though someone else had cut in on my program. I had been using a very sweet, dulcet voice when talking to him under the name of Rosalind, and this time I used a voice that was lower pitched. I've always been good at changing my voice and mimicking people. . . ."

"Go on, go on," Mason said, looking at his watch. "We only have a few minutes.

"I take it you left the envelope with the key for Conway to pick up?"

"That's right."

"Then what did you do?"

"I just framed that murder on him, Mr. Mason. I felt that he could get out of it a lot better than I could. He had money for attorneys' fees, he had position—"

"Well, tell me exactly what you did," Mason said, "so I can get it straightened out."

"Jerry Conway would have recognized me. He had, of course, seen me a good many times. So I put all of this mud on my face and wrapped a towel around my head, and then I took my clothes off."

"Why the clothes off?"

She smiled archly. "Well, I felt that a man wouldn't concentrate so much on my face if he—if I gave him other things to look at."

Mason grinned. "As it turned out, that was pretty good reasoning. Was the body in 729 when Jerry came up there?"

"No, no, I didn't dare take that chance. I thought, of course, I could make him take the gun.

"He fell for my scheme hook, line and sinker. He entered the room, and then I came out and apparently was surprised to see him there. I told him I was Rosalind's

183

roommate, then pretended to get in a panic. I opened the desk and grabbed this gun and cocked it and let my hand keep shaking, and, of course, Jerry Conway did the obvious thing. He was too frightened to do anything else. He grabbed the gun and got out of there."

"And then?" Mason asked.

"Then," she said, "I washed my face, I put on my clothes, I waited until the corridor was empty, and then I tiptoed in and picked up the body. . . . Mr. Mason, it was terrible!"

"You could carry the body all right?" Mason asked.

She said, "I'm strong, Mr. Mason. The girl didn't weigh over a hundred and eighteen pounds, and I had had a course in first aid as a nurse. I got the body as far as the door, and then was the most awful two or three seconds of my life. I had to take that body across the corridor and into Room 729. I just had to take a chance that no one would come up in the elevator, and of course there was a possibility someone might open a room door and come out into the corridor. I had to take that chance, but it was only a few feet, and—well, I made it. You see 729 is a suite, and the door of the bedroom was right opposite the door of 728. I just rushed the body in there, dumped it on the bed, then went back, kicked the bedroom door shut. Then I arranged the body on the bed. After that I stepped out in the corridor and went across to 728 to make sure I hadn't overlooked anything.

"That was when I found the second gun."

"The second gun?"

She nodded and said, "It was under the bed."

"What did you do?"

"I put it in the hatbox. And believe me, after that I went over every inch of that room just as carefully as could be, making certain I had everything cleaned out."

"And then?" Mason asked.

"Then," she said, "I hurried back to put the finishing touch on things in 729. The body had started to stiffen pretty badly. She looked as though she had been dumped on the bed instead of lying the way she should. I just forced her left arm down so it dangled, and moved the head over so the hair was hanging down.

"Then I closed the door, went across the hall to Room 728, and very calmly telephoned the desk and told them to send up a bellboy, I wanted to check out."

"And the bellboy came up?" Mason asked.

"The bellboy came up, and I walked down and checked out. Since Rose had rented the room in the morning, and I was checking out early in the evening, I had to make some explanation. So I told the clerk that my father was critically ill in San Diego and I had to go to him. I said a friend was driving me down. That's all there was to it."

"No, it isn't," Mason said. "What about that second gun?"

She said, "You came here and asked me questions that night, and you remember you said you wanted to use my phone. That phone goes through a switchboard downstairs, and we are charged with calls.

"I was wondering what to do about that gun. After you left, I went downstairs and got the switchboard operator to give me the number you'd called. I called that number and, when the person answered, he said it was the Gladedell Motel. I did some quick thinking and asked him if a Mr. Jerry Conway was registered there, and he said yes, in Unit 21, and did I want him called. I said no, not to call him, that I was just checking, and hung up quick before they could ask any questions.

"So then I waited until after midnight. I drove down to the motel. Jerry Conway's car was parked in front of Unit 21, and I slipped the phony list of stockholders' proxies

185

under the seat of his car, then walked over to the back of the lot. I'd taken a little trowel with me, and I buried that second gun. By that time I didn't know *which* gun had been used in committing the murder. But I felt that if things got to a point where I needed to, I could give the police an anonymous tip, saying I was a woman who lived near the motel and that I'd seen someone burying some metallic object that looked like a gun out there in the lot."

"So," Mason said, "you were willing to have Conway convicted of murder in order to—"

She met his eyes and said, "Mr. Mason, my husband framed me for murder, and believe me, because of the way things went I *was* framed for murder. Don't ever kid yourself, I could have gone to prison for life, or gone to the gas chamber. I had every motive in the world. The murder had been committed with my gun. I had been seen leaving the room where the murdered girl lay. I was up against it. I felt that I could frame enough of a case on Jerry Conway so the police would quit looking for—any other murderer, and I felt absolutely certain that a clever lawyer could keep Jerry Conway from being convicted. I suppose I've been guilty of a crime, and now you've trapped me. I don't know how you found out about all this, but I'm coming clean and I'm throwing myself on your mercy."

Mason looked at his watch and said, "All right, I can't wait any longer. Paul Drake is serving you with a subpoena to appear as a witness for the defense. Serve the subpoena on her, Paul."

Paul Drake handed her a subpoena.

Della Street, who had been taking surreptitious notes, looked up and caught Mason's eye. He raised his eyebrows in silent question, and she nodded, indicating that she had the statement all down.

"All right," Mason said to Drake, "come on, we've got to get back to court."

"You're forgetting one thing," Myrtle Lamar said.

"What?" Mason asked.

"My face," she said. "It's got to be fed."

CHAPTER FIFTEEN

DRIVING BACK to the courthouse, Mason said to Paul Drake, "Paul, this is a damned good lesson in the importance of circumstantial evidence."

"What do you mean?"

"Circumstantial evidence is the best evidence we have," Mason said, "but you have to be careful not to misinterpret it.

"Now, look at the circumstantial evidence of the food in the stomach. Doctors are prepared to state that death took place within approximately two hours of the time the food was ingested. Because they know that the woman in Room 729 had food delivered to her around four-thirty, and presumably started eating when the food was delivered, they placed the time of death at almost exactly six-thirty-five to six-forty-five, the exact time that Jerry Conway was there.

"The only difference is the waiter didn't think there were peas on the dinner menu but peas were found in the stomach of the murder victim. Everyone took it for granted that it was simply a slip-up, a mistake on the part of the waiter in preparing the tray and in remembering what he'd put on there. Actually, it's the most important clue in the whole case. It shows that the woman whose body was found in 729 *couldn't* have been the woman who ordered the dinner which was delivered at four-thirty."

"Well," Drake said, "we knew what happened, but how the devil are you going to prove it? A jury isn't going to believe Mrs. Farrell's story. . . . Or will it?"

"That depends," Mason said, "on how much other evidence we can get. And it depends on who killed Rose Calvert."

"What do you mean?"

"The point that Mrs. Farrell completely missed was that Giff was trying to make it appear that Rose's death was a suicide. He entered the room, he found the body, there wasn't any sign of a gun. That was because the murderer had kicked the murder weapon under the bed—unless he threw it there deliberately. Probably he dropped it and then had kicked it under the bed without knowing what he had done. Or perhaps he just kicked it under the bed hoping it wouldn't be found right away, or not giving a damn and just wanting to get rid of it."

"You mean, you don't think Gifford Farrell is the murderer?"

"The evidence points to the contrary," Mason said. "Why would Gifford Farrell have killed Rose and then discharged another gun into the underside of the mattress so there would be an empty shell in that gun and then have left the gun on the floor by the corpse?"

"So as to implicate his wife," Drake said.

"But don't you see," Mason pointed out, "if he'd done that, he'd have taken the other gun? He wouldn't have left it there."

"Perhaps he didn't know it was there."

"I'm satisfied he didn't know it was there," Mason said. "But *if he had killed* her, he *would* have known it was there, because that was the gun with which she was killed."

"Oh-oh," Drake said. "Now I see your point."

"Therefore," Mason said, "Gifford Farrell was a victim

of circumstances. He tried to make the crime appear a suicide. He was carrying that gun with him, probably for his own protection. He discharged it into the mattress and dropped it by the side of the bed.

"If Mrs. Farrell hadn't got in such a panic, she would have realized that Gifford was trying to set the stage for suicide. He could very easily have told the authorities that this gun was one he had taken home from the Texas Global, that he had given it to Rose for her own protection, that she had become despondent and had committed suicide. But when Mrs. Farrell saw that gun, and saw her husband leaving the room after having heard the shot—which must have been the shot he fired into the underside of the mattress—she became panic-stricken and immediately felt that he was trying to frame the murder on her. So she led with her chin."

"And then she tried to frame it on Conway?"

"That's right," Mason said.

"Well, you can mix the case up all to hell," Drake said, "but the trouble is, Mason, you've got too much of a reputation for mixing things up. The jury is pretty apt to think all this is a big razzle-dazzle, cooked up by a lawyer to mix things up so his client won't be convicted. If you can't shake this damned hotel clerk in his testimony that Rose Calvert was the one who checked into Room 729 claiming she was the secretary for Gerald Boswell, you're hooked."

Mason said, "What I've got to do is to find out what actually happened."

"When do we eat?" Myrtle Lamar asked.

Mason said, "Myrtle, you're going to have to feed your own face."

"What?"

"We'll give you money for the best lunch in town," Mason said, "but we're going to be busy."

She pouted. "That wasn't the way it was promised. Paul

was going to take me to lunch. I want to have lunch with him."

"I have to be in court," Drake said.

"No, you don't. You're not trying the case—and I'll tell you one other thing, you hadn't better leave *me* alone, running around here. I know too much now. You've got to keep me under surveillance, as you detectives call it."

Mason laughed, said, "You win, Myrtle. Paul, you're going to have to take her to lunch."

"But I want to see what happens in court."

"Nothing too much is going to be happening in court," Mason said. "Not right away. The district attorney is stalling, trying to find some way of accounting for that bullet in the underside of the mattress. He wants to prove that I shot it there and he's just about ready to call Inskip so they can lay a foundation to involve me in the case as an accessory.

"So you can count on the fact that he'll stall things along just as much as he can, and this time I'm inclined to play along with him because I want to find out what happened.

"Someone murdered Rose Calvert. I want to find out who."

"Well," Drake said, "don't ever overlook the fact that it could well have been Mrs. Gifford Farrell. She had the room across the corridor from the girl. She hated the girl's guts. She was seen by a chambermaid coming out of the girl's room. . . . Good Lord! Perry, don't let her pull the wool over your eyes by telling a convincing story which, after all, has for its sole purpose getting herself off the hook."

"I'm thinking of that," Mason said.

"And," Drake went on, "she's the one who buried the murder weapon down there at the motel. . . . Hang it, Perry! The more you think of it, the more logical the whole thing becomes. She must have been the one who committed the murder."

"There's just one thing against it," Mason said.

"What?" Drake asked.

"Circumstantial evidence," Mason told him.

"Such as what?"

"Why didn't she give Jerry Conway the murder weapon instead of the weapon that Gifford had planted there to make the death appear suicide?"

Drake tugged at the lobe of his ear for a moment, then said, "Hell's bells, Perry! This is one case I can't figure. Things are coming a little too fast for me. Where do I take Myrtle to lunch?"

"Someplace not too far from the courthouse," Mason said.

"Well, let me out here. This is a darned good restaurant. We'll take a cab and come to court when we're finished. . . . How much of a lunch do you want, Myrtle?"

"Not too much," she said. "I'll have two dry Martinis to start, then a shrimp cocktail, and after that a filet mignon with potatoes au gratin, a little garlic toast, a few vegetables on the side such as asparagus or sweet corn, then some mince pie à la mode, and a big cup of black coffee. That will last me until evening.

"Believe me, it's not very often that one of us girls gets an opportunity to look at the left-hand side of the menu without paying a bit of attention to what's printed on the right-hand side."

Mason glanced at Paul Drake and nodded. "It may be just as well to keep her out of circulation until the situation clarifies itself."

Mason stopped the car and let Paul and Myrtle Lamar out.

"That's a scheming little package," Della Street said when

Mason started the car again. "I hope Paul Drake doesn't get tangled up with her."

"I hope Paul Drake really turns her inside out," Mason said.

"What do you mean? She's turned inside out," Della said.

Mason shook his head. "For all we know, Della, she could have been the one who committed the murder. Anyone around the hotel could."

"Including Bob King?" Della Street asked.

"Including Bob King."

"Well, I'd certainly like to see you wrap it around *his* neck," she said. "But somehow, Chief, I'm inclined to agree with Paul. I think that Mrs. Farrell is mixed in this thing so deep—"

"That's just the point," Mason said. "But then we get back to that business of circumstantial evidence. If she had killed her, she wouldn't have given Jerry Conway the wrong gun."

"What about the gun that did the fatal shooting?" Della asked. "What have they found out about it?"

"So far they haven't told us," Mason said. "But the grapevine has it that they can't tell a thing about the gun, because it was stolen from a hardware store a year and a half ago along with half a dozen other guns.

"Within thirty minutes of the time of the crime, police spotted a car loaded with a bunch of tough-looking kids speeding along. It was about three o'clock in the morning so they took after it. There was quite a chase before they caught the kids. The kids admitted that when they saw the police were taking after them, they threw everything they had taken out of the car windows as they were speeding along. There were half a dozen revolvers, three or four .22 rifles, a lot of ammunition, and some jackknives. Police recovered most of the stuff, but they didn't find a couple of guns, and quite a few of the knives. Almost anyone could have picked up this murder weapon the next day."

"They have the general locality?" Della Street asked.

"That's right."

"Was it near anyplace where Mrs. Farrell would have been?"

"It was at the other end of town," Mason said.

"Well," she told him, "you like circumstantial evidence so much. This is an opportunity to put a jigsaw puzzle together."

"You can put it together two or three different ways," Mason said, "but the pieces don't all fit.

"The trouble with circumstantial evidence isn't with the evidence, but with the reasoning that starts interpreting that evidence. . . . I'm kicking myself over those peas in the dead girl's stomach. There was the most significant clue in the whole case, and damned if I didn't discount it and think it was simply a waiter's mistake.

"I should have cross-examined that waiter up one side and down the other and made him show that he was absolutely positive those peas couldn't have been on the tray taken to 729. I should have made that the big point in the case.

"However, I knew that the peas *were* in the dead girl's stomach and therefore, like everybody else, thought it must have been a mistake on the part of the waiter, and didn't pay too much attention to it."

"Well," Della Street told him, "you've got an assorted set of monkey wrenches now that you can drop into the district attorney's machinery whenever you want to."

"But this time," Mason told her, "I *have* to be right."

They rode up in the elevator to the courtroom and entered just in time to take their seats at the counsel table before court was reconvened.

Judge DeWitt said, "The police officer was on the witness stand."

Elliott, on his feet, said, "If the Court please, I have a few more questions on direct examination to ask of this witness."

"Very well," Judge DeWitt said.

Elliott's questions indicated that he was still sparring for time.

Within ten minutes after court had reconvened, however, the door opened and both Hamilton Burger and Alexander Redfield, the ballistics expert, came tiptoeing into the courtroom.

Redfield took his seat in court, and Hamilton Burger, ponderously tiptoeing forward, reached the counsel table, leaned over and whispered to Elliott.

An expression of beaming good nature was on the district attorney's face.

Elliott listened to Burger's whisper, nodded his head, then said, "That's all. I have no further questions."

"No cross-examination."

Hamilton Burger arose ponderously. "Call Frederick Inskip to the stand."

Inskip came forward and was sworn, and Hamilton Burger, walking around the end of the counsel table to examine him where he would appear to best advantage in front of the jurors, gave every indication of being completely satisfied with the turn of events.

"Mr. Inskip," he said, "what is your occupation? And what was your occupation on the sixteenth and seventeenth of October?"

"A private detective."

"Were you employed on the sixteenth and seventeenth of October by Paul Drake?"

"Yes, sir."

"And on what case were you working?"

"The murder at the Redfern Hotel."

"And did you know who had employed Mr. Drake?"

"Perry Mason."

"How did you know that?"

"I was instructed that Mr. Mason, who was the man in charge of the case, would join me."

"Join you? Where?"

"At the Redfern Hotel."

"You mean you had checked into the Redfern Hotel?"

"I had, yes, sir."

"At what time?"

"Well, it was sometime after the murder. I was instructed to go to the hotel and register in Room 728."

"Why 728? Do you know?"

"I wasn't told."

"But 728 is right across the hall from 729?"

"Yes, sir. The door of 728 is exactly across the hall from the bedroom door of 729. 729 is a suite, and has two doors."

"I see," Hamilton Burger said. "Now, how did you arrange to get in Room 728?"

Judge DeWitt said, "Just a moment. Is this pertinent? This took place *after* the murder was committed. It was a conversation, as I take it, between Paul Drake and a man who was in his employ. It was without the presence of the defendant."

"But," Hamilton Burger said, "we propose to show you, Your Honor, in fact, I think we *have* shown that the conversation was the result of the instructions of Mr. Perry Mason, who was then acting as attorney for the defendant in this case."

Judge DeWitt looked down at Mason and said, "I haven't as yet heard an objection from the defense."

"We have no objection to make, Your Honor," Mason said. "We're quite willing to have any fact in this case that

195

will shed any light on what happened presented to this jury."

"Very well," Judge DeWitt said, "it seeming that there is no objection on the part of the defense, the Court will permit this line of testimony."

"What happened?" Hamilton Burger asked Inskip.

"The phone rang. Paul Drake told me that Mr. Mason, the attorney for whom he was working, would be up, that I was to leave the door unlocked so he could come in without knocking."

"Now, just how did you get Room 728?" Hamilton Burger asked.

"Oh, that was easy. I said I wanted something not too high up and not too low down. They offered me 519 which was vacant. I asked them to see a floor plan of the hotel and said, 'No,' and asked them if they had something perhaps a couple of floors higher up. They said they'd had a check-out in 728 and that was available if I wanted it, and I said I'd take it."

"Now, after receiving that telephone call, what did you do?"

"I left the door unlocked."

"And then what happened?"

"Well, it was about—I'm sorry to say I didn't notice the exact time, but it was around eleven or eleven-thirty—somewhere along there on the morning of the seventeenth that the door opened abruptly and Mr. Mason came in."

"Now you're referring to sometime around eleven o'clock on the morning of October seventeenth?"

"Yes."

"And Mr. Mason entered the room?"

"Yes."

"And what happened?"

"Well, we had some conversation. He asked me to identify myself as working for Drake, and then he asked if I'd looked the room over, and I said I had generally. And he asked if I had a flashlight in my bag."

"And did you have such a flashlight?"

"Yes."

"And then what happened?"

"Mr. Mason looked all around the room carefully with the flashlight, and then he asked me to help him take the sheets and blankets off the bed."

"You did that?"

"Yes, sir."

"Then what happened?"

"Then he raised the mattress and found a bullet hole in the underside of the mattress."

There was an audible, collective gasp from spectators in the courtroom.

Judge DeWitt leaned forward. "A bullet hole?" he asked.

"Yes, sir."

"How do you know it was a bullet hole?" Judge DeWitt asked sharply.

"Because working together, we got the bullet out of the hole."

"How did you get it out?" Hamilton Burger asked.

"We cut a wire coat hanger to pieces and made an instrument that would get the bullet out. First we probed and found there was a bullet in there, and then we got the bullet out."

"And what happened to that bullet?"

"I kept it in my possession."

"Did you mark the bullet so you could identify it?"

"Yes, sir."

"At whose suggestion?"

"At Mr. Mason's suggestion."

"I show you a bullet and ask you if that was the bullet which you extracted from the mattress?"

The witness looked at the bullet and said, "It is."

"Do you know how Mr. Mason knew that bullet hole was in the mattress?" Hamilton Burger asked.

"No, sir."

"But he did suggest to you that there might well be something in the mattress?"

"Yes, sir."

"And asked you to help him remove the blankets and sheets?"

"Yes, sir."

"And then he turned up the mattress?"

"Yes, sir."

"And indicated this bullet hole with his flashlight?"

"Yes, sir."

Hamilton Burger smiled triumphantly. "That's all."

"No questions on cross-examination," Mason said.

Hamilton Burger seemed somewhat nonplused by Mason's attitude.

"Call Alexander Redfield," Burger said.

Alexander Redfield came forward.

"I show you the bullet which has been identified by the witness Inskip," Hamilton Burger said. "Do you know what gun discharged that bullet?"

"Yes, sir."

"What gun?"

"A Smith & Wesson gun, numbered C 48809."

"A gun which has previously been introduced in evidence here?"

"Yes, sir."

"The gun which the defendant Conway admitted he had in his possession?"

"Yes, sir."

"Now then," Hamilton Burger said, "there are two bullets in this case, and two guns."

"Yes, sir."

"There is a Colt, numbered 740818?"

"Yes, sir."

"And a bullet was fired from that gun?"

"Yes, sir."

"And what bullet was that?"

"That was the fatal bullet."

"That was the bullet that was given you by the autopsy surgeon as having been the bullet which caused the death of Rose Calvert?"

"Yes, sir."

"And that bullet was fired from that Colt revolver?"

"Yes, sir."

"And this bullet which you have now identified is a bullet which was fired from the Smith & Wesson, the one which is received in evidence and which bears the number C 48809. This is the same gun which the evidence shows Mr. Conway, the defendant in this case, produced and handed to the authorities as being the gun which he claimed had been pointed at him in Room 729 and which he had taken away from this mysterious woman whom he had described in such detail?"

"Yes, sir."

"That's all," Hamilton Burger said.

"No cross-examination," Mason said.

Judge DeWitt frowned at Mason.

"I'm going to recall Robert King," Hamilton Burger said.

King came forward and took the witness stand.

"You have already been sworn," the district attorney said. "I am going to ask you what the hotel records show in regard to Room 728."

"It was rented to a Ruth Culver."

"And what happened to Ruth Culver?"

"She checked out of the hotel at about six-fifty on the evening of October sixteenth."

"When did she rent the room?"

"Around ten o'clock in the morning of October six-teenth."

"Who checked her out?"

"I presented her with the bill, which she paid in cash."

"And then what?"

"It was early enough to have the room made up so we could rerent it again if we needed to that night."

"Cross-examine," Hamilton Burger said.

Mason said, "You didn't see Ruth Culver when she checked in, did you?"

"No, sir."

"You weren't on duty at that time?"

"No, sir."

"So for all you know, the woman who checked out of Room 728 may not have been the same woman who registered in there?"

"I know she was the woman who checked out of 728."

"How do you know that?"

"Because she paid the bill, and the bellboy went up and brought the baggage down."

"Quite right. You know some woman checked out of Room 728 but you don't know it was the same woman who checked in, do you?"

"Well, I didn't see her when she checked in. I wasn't on duty."

"For all you know of your own knowledge," Mason said, "the woman who rented 728 could well have been Rose Calvert, whose body was found in Room 729."

"Oh, Your Honor," Hamilton Burger said, "I object to this question. It is argumentative. It is completely incompetent, irrelevant, and immaterial, and it shows the straws at which counsel is clutching."

"The question *is* argumentative," Judge DeWitt said.

"If the Court please," Mason said, "it is a logical question. The initials of Ruth Culver and Rose Calvert are the same. The baggage which was taken down from 728 and the initials 'R.C.' and—"

"Your Honor, Your Honor!" Hamilton Burger shouted. "I object to this statement. I assign the making of it as misconduct. I point out to the court that the whole specious, fabricated nature of this defense is now coming into court in its true light.

"The defendant in this case admittedly had the Smith & Wesson revolver in his possession from around six-thirty-five on the evening of the sixteenth until it was surrendered to the officers on the morning of the seventeenth.

"The defendant had consulted Perry Mason as his attorney, and presumably had turned the gun over to him. At least he had the opportunity to do so.

"Mr. Mason, finding out that there had been a check-out on the seventh floor of the hotel during the evening, had ample opportunity to get to that room to fire a shot in the mattress, then instruct a detective to go to that room and be there so that Mr. Mason could make a grandstand of *discovering* the bullet hole in the mattress the next morning.

"This is evidence of unprofessional conduct on the part of counsel. It makes him an accessory after the fact—"

"Now, just a minute! Just a minute!" Judge DeWitt interrupted, banging his gavel down on the desk. "We'll have no accusations of this nature at this time, Mr. District Attorney. You have objected to the question on the ground that it is argumentative. In the light of Mr. Mason's statement, it is now the opinion of the Court that the question is *not* argumentative. Counsel is simply asking the witness what is a self-evident fact, that since the witness doesn't know who checked into Room 728, it could have been anybody. It could have been the young woman who was subsequently found murdered. It could have been anyone.

"Now, the Court suggests that, if you want to show who this person was who checked into Room 728, if it becomes important for any reason, you can produce that person and have her testify, or in the event you can't produce her, and any attempt is made to show that the person who checked into 728 was the person whose body was found in 729, you can produce the register and have a handwriting expert testify as to the differences in handwriting."

Mason grinned and said, "And when he does that, Your Honor, the handwriting expert will have to testify that the Ruth Culver who signed the register and checked into 728 was the Rose Calvert whose body was found in 729."

"Your Honor! Your Honor!" Hamilton Burger shouted. "This is improper. That is an improper statement. That is misconduct on the part of defense counsel."

"Well," Judge DeWitt said, "let's not have so much excitement about this. After all, the matter is perfectly obvious. Have you checked the registration, Mr. District Attorney?"

Hamilton Burger's face purpled. "No, Your Honor, we haven't because there is no need for so doing. We don't need to check the handwriting of every person who registered in the Redfern Hotel on the morning of the sixteenth in order to negative some perfectly fallacious theory which the defense is trying to advance."

"Well, if you're not going to anticipate the defense, and call witnesses to refute it in advance," Judge DeWitt said, "I fail to see the reason for calling the witness Inskip."

"We want to show the tactics of defense counsel."

"Well, go ahead and show them," Judge DeWitt said, "but refrain from personalities, and if I were you, Mr. Prosecutor, I would put on my own case, and then in the event defense makes any claims, you have an opportunity to call witnesses in rebuttal. It always is a dangerous practice to try and anticipate a defense and negative it in advance, and it is not in accordance with the best practice.

"Proceed with the cross-examination of this witness, Mr. Mason."

"No further cross-examination," Mason said.

"Call your next witness," Judge DeWitt said to Hamilton Burger.

"I will call Norton Barclay Calvert, the husband of the dead woman," Hamilton Burger said. "Come forward, Mr. Calvert, and be sworn."

There was a moment's delay while the bailiff's voice could be heard outside of the courtroom calling Norton Calvert.

A few moments later the door opened and Norton Calvert entered the courtroom and came forward to the witness stand.

He took the oath, settled himself on the witness stand, and Hamilton Burger said, "Your name is Norton Barclay Calvert, and you are the surviving husband of Rose M. Calvert?"

"Yes, sir."

"You have identified the body of Rose Calvert? You saw that in the morgue?"

"Yes, sir."

"When did you first know that your wife was dead?"

Mason said, "That is objected to, if the Court please, on the ground that it's incompetent, irrelevant, and immaterial. It makes no difference to the issues in this case when he first knew his wife was dead."

Judge DeWitt nodded his head.

"Just a moment, before the Court rules," Hamilton Burger said. "May I be heard?"

"Certainly, Mr. Prosecutor."

"We propose to show by this witness," Burger said, "that he was appraised early in the morning of the seventeenth that his wife had been murdered, that this was long before the police knew the identity of the body. We propose to show that he was advised by Mr. Perry Mason, who was acting as attorney for the defendant, and that the only way Mr. Mason could possibly have known the identity of the murdered woman was by having his client give him that information. And the only way his client could have secured the information was by seeing and recognizing the murdered woman."

Judge DeWitt looked at Mason. "That would seem to put something of a different aspect on the situation, Mr. Mason."

"How is he going to prove that the only way I had of knowing the identity of the murdered woman was because of something my client told me?" Mason asked.

"We'll prove it by inference," Hamilton Burger said.

"I think there is no necessity for having any further discussion on this matter," Judge DeWitt said. "I dislike to have offers of proof made in front of the jury. I think the testimony of the witness will speak for itself, but under the circumstances the Court is going to overrule the objection."

"When did you first know that your wife had been murdered?" Hamilton Burger asked.

"About one o'clock on the morning of the seventeenth."

"Where were you?"

"At my home in Elsinore."

"How did you find out your wife was dead?"

"Mr. Mason told me she had been murdered."

"By Mr. Mason, you mean Perry Mason, the attorney for the defendant here?"

"Yes, sir."

"Now, let's not have any misunderstanding about this," Hamilton Burger said. "You learned of your wife's death through a statement made by Perry Mason to the effect that she had been murdered, and that statement was made around one o'clock in the morning of October seventeenth in Elsinore, California?"

"Yes, sir."

"Cross-examine!" Hamilton Burger snapped at Perry Mason.

"Do you remember what time I got to your house?" Mason asked.

"I think it was about twelve-forty-five or so."

"Do you know when I left?"

"I know that you had left by a quarter past one," he said. "You were there about half an hour, I think."

"Didn't I tell you that I thought your wife had been murdered after I had looked at pictures of your wife?"

"I showed you some pictures, but you seemed pretty positive. Otherwise you wouldn't have gone down to see me at that hour in the morning."

Hamilton Burger grinned.

Judge DeWitt rebuked the witness. "Kindly refrain from arguing with counsel. Simply answer questions."

"Yes, sir, that's what you told me, but you woke me up out of a sound sleep in the middle of the night to tell me."

"I woke you up?"

"Yes."

"You had been sleeping?"

"I was sound asleep."

"You went to bed when?"

"Nine-thirty or ten."

"Had no trouble getting to sleep?"

"Certainly not."

"And slept soundly until I came?"

"Yes."

"Hadn't got up even to take a smoke?"

"No."

"You know as a heavy smoker that about the first thing

a smoker does on awakening is to reach for a cigarette?"

"Certainly."

"Yet after you let me in, you sat there for five minutes before you had a cigarette, didn't you?"

"I . . . I don't remember that so well. I had been—I can't recall."

Mason said, "Didn't I tell you, Mr. Calvert, that I got your address from a letter which you had written your wife?"

"I don't remember," Calvert said. "I was pretty much broken up, and I don't remember too much about what you said about how you got there, but I remember you came there and told me my wife had been murdered."

"You had written your wife a letter, hadn't you?"

"Objected to as incompetent, irrelevant, and immaterial and not proper cross-examination," Hamilton Burger said. "My interrogation was only as to a conversation with Mr. Mason. If Mr. Mason wants to make this man his own witness, he can do so."

"It is entirely proper to show the attitude of the witness and possible bias on the part of the witness," Judge DeWitt said. "I don't see what difference it makes."

"Well," Mason said, "in order to come within the technical rules of evidence, I'll reframe the question and ask him if he didn't *tell* me that he had written his wife a letter?"

"I don't remember. I think I did."

"And," Mason said, "isn't it a fact that your wife, Rose Calvert, wrote and told you that she wanted to go to Reno and get a divorce?"

"Yes."

"That she wanted you to hire counsel to represent you so you could make things easier for her?"

"Yes."

"And when I rang the doorbell early on the morning of

the seventeenth of October and told you that I wanted to talk with you about your wife, that I was an attorney, didn't you tell me that you wouldn't consent to anything, that you wouldn't do anything to make it easier for her to get a divorce?"

"Yes."

"And didn't you tell me that you had answered the letter she had written and told her something to that effect?"

"I believe I did, yes."

"And didn't I tell you that that letter was in the mailbox at her apartment?"

"I don't remember."

"Oh yes, you do," Mason said.

"The reason you didn't go to the Elsinore police station to find out if your wife had been murdered until considerably later on the morning of the seventeenth was that you suddenly realized that this letter you had mailed your wife would direct suspicion to you. You had told your wife in that letter that you would kill her before you'd let her marry anyone else, didn't you?"

The witness looked at Mason with sullen hostility, then slowly shook his head.

"No, I didn't say anything like that."

"And," Mason said, "the minute I told you that letter was in the mailbox, you knew that that was a clue pointing toward you that you had forgotten, and that you had to go in and get that letter out of the mailbox before you asked the police to find out if your wife had been murdered."

"That's not true!"

Mason, frowning thoughtfully, turned to survey the courtroom, studying the faces of the spectators.

At that moment the door opened, and Paul Drake and Myrtle Lamar entered the courtroom.

Mason said, "If the Court please, I notice that Myrtle Lamar has just entered the courtroom. I would like to ask Miss Lamar to come forward and stand by me for a moment. And I would like to ask the witness to arise."

"What's the reason for all this?" Hamilton Burger asked.

"Myrtle Lamar," Mason said, "as one of the elevator operators at the Redfern Hotel, has her own means of making an identification of persons who go up in the elevator. Kindly step forward, Miss Lamar."

Mason moved over to the swinging gate which divided the bar from the courtroom and said, "Right this way, please."

Myrtle Lamar moved through the gate.

"I object," Hamilton Burger said.

"On what grounds?" Judge DeWitt asked.

"He can't examine two witnesses at once," Hamilton Burger said.

"He's not trying to," Judge DeWitt said. "He is, as I understand it, trying to make an identification."

"If the Court please," Mason said, "I feel that perhaps I do owe Court and counsel an explanation. It seems that Miss Lamar makes a point of studying the feet of the persons who go up and down in the elevators. I notice that this witness has a peculiar habit of turning his right foot in at a sharp angle. I also notice he is wearing a distinctive shoe, a high-laced shoe with a heavy box-toe cap. I believe these shoes are advertised by one of the well-known mail-order houses as being ideal for service-station attendants in that they will not slip and are resistant to oil and gasoline."

Mason turned back to the witness. "Stand up, please."

Calvert sullenly got to his feet.

"Now, just a minute, just a minute," Hamilton Burger said, pushing back from his chair and lumbering toward the witness. "I want to see this."

Mason said to Calvert, "You're holding your right foot

so the toe is pointed straight ahead. Do you always stand that way?"

"Of course," Calvert said.

Abruptly Myrtle Lamar started to laugh. "That's not true," she said in a loud, clear voice. "I'd never forget those shoes. When he stands relaxed, his right toe is pointed in. He's deliberately holding it—"

"Order!" Judge DeWitt shouted. "You will not give any testimony at this time, Miss Lamar. You are being brought up here purely for the purpose of identification. You will now return to your seat in the courtroom. The witness will resume his seat in the witness chair."

Hamilton Burger said, "Your Honor, I object. I move all of this statement be stricken as not being the statement of a witness, and—"

"The motion is granted!" Judge DeWitt snapped. "Mr. Mason can, of course, call Miss Lamar as his witness if he desires, but her statement will be stricken from the evidence."

"Sit down," Mason said to Calvert.

Mason stood for a moment, looking at the witness with searching eyes. Then he said in a tone that was not without sympathy, "You loved your wife, didn't you, Calvert?"

Calvert nodded.

"You felt you couldn't live without her. You wanted her to come back to you."

The witness was silent.

"And," Mason said, "you made up your mind that if you couldn't have her, no one else was going to have her. You were willing to kill her and probably intended to kill yourself at the same time. Then you lost your nerve and didn't go through with the suicide."

The witness shifted his position uncomfortably. For a swift moment his lips twisted on a choking sob, then he regained control of himself.

Mason said, "If the Court please, I feel that the circumstances are highly unusual. I would like to have a ten-minute recess so that I can interview certain witnesses."

"I object to any continuance at this time," Hamilton Burger said in sputtering protest.

"Is it absolutely necessary to have a recess at this time in order to interview these witnesses, Mr. Mason?" Judge DeWitt asked.

"It is, Your Honor. Mrs. Farrell was having detectives shadow Rose Calvert's apartment. I can't say for certain what time these detectives went off duty on the night of the sixteenth and the morning of the seventeenth, but I am hoping that one of these detectives can testify that this witness was seen going to the mailbox and taking this incriminating letter he had written out of the mailbox so the police wouldn't find it when they came to search the apartment after the body had been identified."

"Your Honor, I object to these statements being made in front of the jury," Hamilton Burger said. "This is simply a grandstand—"

"Counsel will refrain from personalities," Judge DeWitt said sharply. "The Court has previously stated that it dislikes to have offers of proof made in front of the jury. However, this statement was in response to a question asked by the Court itself, and the question was prompted by the fact that the prosecution objected to the recess. The Court feels that under the peculiar circumstances it is only fair to grant the motion, and Court will take a ten-minute recess."

Mason hurried through the swinging gate in the bar to Paul Drake. "Put a shadow on Calvert," he said.

Drake said, "Perry, you know those detectives went off duty at around one-thirty on the morning of the seventeenth. There was no one there to see Calvert take that letter, and—"

Mason said in a low voice, "In poker, Paul, you some-

210

times shove in a stack of blue chips when you only have a pair of deuces in your hand. Get busy and follow Calvert. *I* think he's going to skip out."

Calvert, walking doggedly toward the door, was suddenly confronted by Myrtle Lamar. She said, "You know good and well that I took you up in the elevator on the sixteenth, the day of the murder, and I took you down again. When we got to the seventh floor you asked me—"

Suddenly Calvert shoved her out of the way and started running through the door of the courtroom and pell-mell down the corridor.

"Stop him!" someone screamed. "Stop that man!"

Two spectators tried to grab Calvert. He engaged in a wild struggle with them. Officers ran up and grabbed the man's arms. His wrists were handcuffed behind his back.

There was pandemonium in the corridor.

CHAPTER SIXTEEN

MASON, DELLA STREET, Paul Drake, Jerry Conway, and Myrtle Lamar sat in the courtroom after the commotion had subsided, after the judge had instructed the jury to bring in a verdict of "Not Guilty" in the case against Jerry Conway, after Calvert had been taken into custody.

"Where did you get the bright idea of what had happened?" Paul Drake asked Mason.

"That," Mason said, "was the simplest part of it, the mathematics of the whole business which had been in the back of my mind but didn't come out until something suddenly clicked.

"The pathologist stated that Rose had died almost two

hours to the minute after she had eaten lunch. He thought that lunch had been eaten at four-forty. Actually we know from Mrs. Farrell that lunch had been eaten at about twelve-forty. That fixed the time of death at about two-forty. At that particular time Mrs. Farrell was out telephoning you, Conway.

"I suddenly remembered that I had told Calvert about locating him from the return address on the letter that was in the mailbox of the apartment house where Rose was living. Yet the police told us no such letter was in the box when they searched the place. Shortly after I told Calvert about the letter, he went all to pieces and insisted that I leave him alone. I felt certain that he would go to the Elsinore police almost immediately. He didn't. He didn't get in touch with them until sometime later, just about enough time for him to go and get that letter.

"The rest of it was just plain bluff, based on Myrtle's noticing the guy's shoes."

"Well," Jerry Conway said at length, "I'm going to ask you to appear before the stockholders' meeting, Mason, and tell them the whole story of this murder case. Will you do it?"

Mason nodded.

"I have an idea," Conway said, "that *that* will settle Gifford Farrell's hash as far as any attempt to take over is concerned."

Mason turned to Drake with a grin, and said, "Well, Paul, having bought Myrtle Lamar a good lunch, I think we now owe her a good dinner."

Myrtle Lamar's eyes instantly became hard and calculating. "It should be worth more than that," she said. "It should be worth a . . . a fur coat!"

Jerry Conway grinned happily, said to Perry Mason, "Buy the gal a fur coat, Perry, and charge it to me. . . . Put it on your fee as an expense."